Three Screams!
You're Out!

Buddy Sanders only wants to play ball on a team that doesn't stink. But when he makes that wish on Fear Street, Buddy gets more than he bargained for.

He's sent back in time—way back—to play on the best Shadyside team ever. And he doesn't know how to get home.

There's one other catch—the team is doomed. Doomed to be caught in a horrible bus accident. Can Buddy make it back to the future before the big crash?

Or has he really struck out this time?

Also from R.L. Stine

The Beast®
The Beast® 2

R.L. Stine's Ghosts of Fear Street
#1 Hide and Shriek
#2 Who's Been Sleeping in My Grave?
#3 The Attack of the Aqua Apes
#4 Nightmare in 3-D
#5 Stay Away from the Tree House
#6 Eye of the Fortuneteller
#7 Fright Knight
#8 The Ooze
#9 Revenge of the Shadow People
#10 The Bugman Lives
#11 The Boy Who Ate Fear Street
#12 Night of the Werecat
#13 How to Be a Vampire
#14 Body Switchers from Outer Space
#15 Fright Christmas
#16 Don't Ever Get Sick at Granny's
#17 House of a Thousand Screams
#18 Camp Fear Ghouls
#19 Three Evil Wishes
#20 Spell of the Screaming Jokers
#21 The Creature from Club Lagoona

Available from MINSTREL Books

FIELD OF SCREAMS

A Parachute Press Book

A MINSTREL® BOOK

PUBLISHED BY POCKET BOOKS

New York   London   Toronto   Sydney   Tokyo   Singapore

A MINSTREL PAPERBACK *Original*

 A Minstrel Paperback published by
POCKET BOOKS, a division of Simon & Schuster Inc.
1230 Avenue of the Americas, New York, NY 10020

Copyright © 1997 by Parachute Press, Inc.

FIELD OF SCREAMS WRITTEN BY P. MacFEARSON

ISBN: 0-671-00851-X

First Minstrel Books paperback printing July 1997

10 9 8 7 6 5 4 3 2 1

FEAR STREET is a registered trademark of Parachute Press, Inc.

A MINSTREL BOOK and colophon are registered trademarks of
Simon & Schuster Inc.

Cover art by Broeck Steadman

Printed in the U.S.A.

I stood with the bat over my shoulder and the ball in my left hand. I narrowed my eyes and glared down the field at my friend Eve.

"Are you ready for a hot one?" I yelled.

"You couldn't hit a hot one with a big old frying pan, Sanders!" Eve teased me. "You're such a weenie!"

"Weenie, huh?" I retorted. I ran my hand through my curly brown hair. I dug my foot into the dirt to get a good stance. Shifting my balance, I lofted the ball and hit a screaming grounder straight at Eve.

She went down with her glove and tried to stop it. But the ball took a wicked hop and skipped right through her mitt.

"Who's the weenie now, butterfingers?" I yelled.

The ball stopped about ten feet behind Eve. Her dark braids bounced as she jogged over and snatched it up. "You hit it weird, Buddy," she complained, throwing it back. "The next one won't get by me!"

I plucked the baseball easily from the air. "Those balls get by you so much, I think your glove is made of Swiss cheese!"

"Lay off, okay?" Eve grumbled.

Sometimes, I guess, I tease her a little too much.

"You took your eyes off the ball," I reminded her. "Remember what Coach Burress says. Follow the ball into your glove."

I hit another to her, not quite so hard this time.

Eve missed it. Again.

I shook my head. I'd been trying to help Eve with her fielding for three weeks, but it was no use. I had to face the facts. Eve was an awesome friend. But she was a lousy ballplayer.

The trouble was, *everybody* on the Shadyside Middle School baseball team was lousy. Everybody but me. And I was sick of it.

Just once, I thought as Eve ran over to the ball. Just once I'd like to play on a really good team. Is that too much to ask?

But no. This was our team's third season—and it smelled like another loser.

I felt bad about being annoyed at Eve. It wasn't her fault she couldn't play. She always tried her best. She was great at soccer and basketball. But baseball just wasn't in her.

"Sorry, Buddy," she called. "I'll get it next time."

"Sure. I'll hit you some flies for a while." Eve was pretty good at catching those.

And at least I was doing my favorite thing in the world—playing ball. School was out for the summer, and for once my mom didn't have any chores for me to do. Like mowing the grass or cleaning out the garage.

Eve and I were playing in an empty field that backed onto some of the older houses on Fear Street. These tall gray houses towered up above high wooden fences. They looked menacing and spooky. There was one in particular that got to me. It had dark windows like eyes that watched us play.

I was careful hitting the ball. I didn't want to have to go find it in one of those yards.

Not that Fear Street scared me. Sure, I'd heard all those stories about it—about ghosts in the cemetery and weird things in Fear Lake. But I didn't believe them.

Well, not really.

The more I hit the ball to Eve, the more that gloomy old house bothered me. Was someone really watching me behind those windows? It felt like it.

I tossed the ball up again and gave another swing. My aluminum bat connected with a *clang*.

The ball leapt off the bat like a rocket. I stared at it in surprise. I didn't realize I had taken such a big swing.

The ball shot through the air as if Cecil Fielder hit it. Eve craned her neck to watch it sail over her head.

"Oh, no!" I yelled. The ball disappeared over the fence.

Right into the one place I hoped it wouldn't go.

The backyard of that spooky house on Fear Street.

2

I stared at the creepy old house for a second.

Then I sprinted over to Eve. I'm short, but I move fast. I reached her in a few seconds.

"Wow!" she said as I ran up. "You really nailed that ball. No way could I have hit one that far!"

I just shrugged. I don't usually hit them that far either. But I wasn't about to admit that.

We jogged toward the fence. Its cedar boards stood warped with age. There were lots of holes to look through. I cupped my hands around my eyes to peek into the yard.

"Do you see the ball?" Eve asked.

"Nope," I answered. "Just a bunch of old junk."

I stepped back and studied the fence. I found a

place where the boards were loose. I shoved them aside.

"What are you doing?" Eve asked nervously.

"I'm going in to find my ball," I told her.

"Forget it, Buddy," Eve urged. "This place is creepy."

I rolled my eyes. "You don't believe all that Fear Street stuff, do you?"

Eve's cheeks turned red. "Don't you?"

"Hah! No way!" I said as I squeezed through the gap in the fence.

Well, I didn't. Not really.

"What a mess," I muttered as I looked the place over. Old pieces of machinery and broken furniture lay everywhere. No grass or trees grew. Just dirt and a few weeds here and there.

I glanced up at the house. Eve was right. It was pretty gruesome. Just the kind of place you'd expect a ghost or monster to live in. That is, if you believed in ghosts or monsters.

"Hurry up, Buddy," Eve whispered through the fence.

I moved toward the back porch. It was built up off the ground about three feet. I bent to peek underneath. Nothing but piled-up leaves and dirt. But then I caught a glimpse of white. Way back under the porch. My ball!

I got on my hands and knees and crawled after it. The day was so bright that when I ducked under the porch into the darkness I couldn't see a thing. I blinked a few times, and my eyes adjusted.

"Gross," I said as I moved forward. A horrible stink invaded my nose. It smelled like a sewer. I saw a big pipe way in the back with a crack in it. Thick brown goo seeped out.

I pinched my nose shut. The sooner you get the ball, the sooner you can get out of here, I thought. I started toward it again. Something sticky brushed against my forehead.

I reached up and pulled at whatever it was.

Ugh! A clump of cobweb came off in my hand. I reached up again to feel my hair. Webs stuck to it in thick gobs.

Something tickled the back of my neck. I swiped at it. A spider fell from my neck to the ground. "Oh, man," I moaned.

Then I felt more tickling. Like things moving in my hair, crawling across my ears. I swatted at them.

Dozens of little spiders swarmed over my fingers!

I fell flat on the ground, slapping at my head with both hands. "Get off me!" I yelled. "Get off me!"

When I was pretty sure I'd gotten rid of them all, I breathed a sigh of relief.

What am I, nuts? I thought. Who cares about the baseball? I have another one at home. This place is bad news. I'm leaving.

But then I glanced ahead of me. The ball was within reach. All I had to do was grab it.

7

I stretched out as far as I could. My fingertips touched the ball. I rolled it toward me. I almost had it. . . .

Something cold and hard suddenly locked around my ankle. "Yipe!" I squawked, and tried to jerk away.

Whatever had me held on tight. I felt it pulling at me. I kicked with my free foot. But the grip was like iron!

It dragged me backward. I fought as hard as I could. But it was no use. I was helpless.

I was caught!

3

I slid backward so fast, my face scraped against the dirt. I tried to yell, but dry leaves filled my mouth.

Then bright sunlight hit my face, blinding me. I blinked hard, trying to make my eyes adjust, but they wouldn't. Whatever had me in its clutches, I couldn't see it. The thing grabbed my shoulder. I felt myself being lifted up off the ground.

Finally, my eyes began to focus. I lifted my head and stared into the face of a wrinkled old man. He gazed down at me with cold, dark eyes. Only a few wisps of gray hair dotted his bald head. His lips parted, and I could see stained, yellowed teeth.

He was holding me three feet above the ground. His hands clamped my shoulders like vises. I squirmed, trying to get loose, but he hung on. Talk about strong!

"What are you doing under my house? You looking for something?" he demanded in a hoarse, rough voice.

"Let me down. Ow! Let me down!" I yelled. My heart pounded in my ears. What did this old man want with me?

Then, all of sudden, he let go. I fell to the ground and tumbled in the dirt.

"Ow!" I glared at him. "You didn't have to do that."

The man's lined face crinkled up like old paper as he grinned. He seemed to think I was funny.

"It's dangerous under that porch. I couldn't let you crawl under there. Besides, how do I know you're not trying to rob me? How do I know you aren't some kind of thief?"

"I am not a thief!" I protested. "I was just trying to get my baseball back. I got up and brushed the dirt from my pants and shirt. "I hit it over the fence by accident, and it rolled under your porch."

The old man's eyes narrowed. He scratched his chin.

"Baseball, huh?"

"It's the truth. I almost had it, when you grabbed me. If you don't believe me, look for yourself."

"I think I'll just do that," he said.

The old man grunted and crouched down on his hands and knees. He was wearing old, faded slacks and a suit jacket that dragged in the dirt as he peered under the porch.

He stuck his whole head underneath.

Maybe the spiders would get him, I thought. It would serve him right for scaring me.

He reached a hand back toward me, his head still under the porch. "Fetch me that rake by the wall."

I brought the old iron rake and put the handle in his hand. He stuck it under the porch and began to poke around.

"As I was saying, these old houses are dangerous, boy," he called up to me. He was under the porch up to his shoulders now. His bony rear stuck up in the air. "There's all kinds of stuff under here. Old rusty metal, black widow spiders . . ."

"Tell me about it," I muttered under my breath.

The old man started backing out. He drew out the rake. My baseball came with it. "There you go, son," he said, handing me the ball. "Next time, try fishing the ball out like I did, instead of diving under a stranger's porch without thinking."

I felt embarrassed now. Maybe he wasn't such a bad old guy after all.

"I guess you're right," I admitted. "Uh—thanks for getting my ball."

"What's your name, son?" the old man asked.

"Buddy Sanders," I answered.

"Ernie Ames. Call me Ernie," the old man said. He extended his hand to shake.

I grabbed it. It felt hard and scratchy, like sandpaper. I pulled my hand away fast. I hoped he didn't notice.

I glanced back at the fence. Was Eve still watching?

"So you're a ballplayer, eh? You on a team?" he asked.

"Sure. I play third base for the Shadyside team."

Ernie grinned. "That's not a team. That's a joke."

"Aw, we do all right." I felt myself blush.

"Really? Won any games lately?"

I stared down at the dirt and dug around with my toe. "Well—not really."

"That's what I thought," he said.

I scowled. Okay, so it was a bonehead move for me to crawl under the guy's porch. But he didn't have to insult my team.

"So what?" I argued. "Just because the team isn't very good doesn't mean it isn't fun. And I can be a good third baseman even if my team doesn't always win."

Ernie's lips curled in a mean smile. "So you think you're pretty good, huh? Aren't you kind of short for a ballplayer?"

He was making me mad! I guess that's why I started bragging.

"Maybe I am short. But I'm good," I declared. "Coach thinks I'm the best third baseman he's ever had. Maybe the best ever to play for Shadyside."

"Impossible!" Ernie snorted. "Gibson was the best third baseman ever to play for Shadyside. Buddy

Gibson. He had it all—the glove, the bat . . ." He stared off into the distance as if he were remembering.

"Oh, yeah? Then how come I never heard of him?" I sneered.

The old man's gaze snapped back to mine. His eyes suddenly looked like two holes. Dark. Empty.

"Because for all his talent, Buddy Gibson was unlucky."

His voice sent chills through me. "Wh-what do you mean?"

Ernie leaned in close and whispered, "Buddy Gibson—and his whole team—were in the wrong place at the wrong time.

"And now they're buried in the Fear Street Cemetery!"

4

Buried in the Fear Street Cemetery?

I sucked in my breath. "You—you mean they all . . ."

Ernie Ames nodded.

"What happened to them?" I asked.

His face twisted as if he were in pain. "They were called the Doom Squad," he said slowly. "Folks called them that because they beat everybody. To play them meant doom. But once I—I mean once *they* had their accident, well—then they really *were* the Doom Squad. They all died. Every single one of them."

I shuddered. A whole baseball team—dead!

"What accident?" I asked. "How did it happen?"

Ernie turned without answering. He shuffled to the porch steps. "Wait here," he said.

"But—" I started to say.

Too late. He'd already gone inside. I ran over to the fence.

"Eve? Eve? Are you still there?" I called.

No one answered. Eve must have run off.

"Weenie," I muttered.

Should I take off myself? Ernie kind of gave me the creeps. On the other hand, I was curious about this Doom Squad.

Before I could make up my mind, Ernie came back out of the house. He shuffled down the porch steps, holding a shoe box. "Here we go," he said. "I've been saving these for years."

He pulled an old, creased paper from the box. I took it from him and stared at it. An old black-and-white picture of a kids' baseball team. Twelve guys—no girls. All about my age, twelve.

"That's the Doom Squad," Ernie explained. He moved behind me and pointed over my shoulder to different players.

"That one's Jimmy Grogan, the first baseman. Wade Newsom—he was the pitcher. Fielders Boog Johnson, Chad Weems, and Johnny Beans. Catcher, Billy Fein."

I checked the picture out. Everyone looked funny in their baggy, pin-striped uniforms. Their hats had little crowns with long bills. They look more like the *duck* squad than the Doom Squad, I thought.

"Which one is this Gibson kid?" I asked.

"That one." The old man's finger trembled as he pointed. "That's Gibson."

Buddy Gibson stared out of the photograph with a wide grin. He seemed more comfortable than the others, like he'd been born in that uniform.

Ernie must have guessed what I was thinking. "Looks like he belongs on a baseball card, doesn't he? Well, he did. Every player on that team was good, but Buddy was special. He had the real stuff. He was going to the majors."

I shifted uncomfortably. Did Ernie have to stand so close? His clothes had a funny, musty smell. Like they'd been sprinkled with soil or something.

"What year was this taken?" I asked.

"Nineteen forty-eight. Their last year. Right before the championship game."

"Did they win?" I asked.

"That's where the unluckiness comes in. They lost," the old man explained. "It was the bottom of the ninth. Bases were loaded and there were two outs. Shadyside led by two runs."

I nodded. I could picture it.

"A left-handed hitter came up to the plate. The coach moved everybody over, expecting him to hit the ball to the right, but he didn't. He hit a line drive to the left, down the third base line. It was a triple. Three runs scored. And Shadyside lost."

"Wow! That is a tough break," I agreed. "But why did it land them in the cemetery?"

"Losing the championship was only the beginning. There was supposed to be a party after the game for everyone—the winners and the losers. But the Doom Squad was so disappointed, they just left. On the way home their bus stalled on the railroad tracks. An oncoming train hit the bus. Killed them all."

"That's awful!" I gasped.

Ernie's lips were clamped tight. I didn't know what to say. He probably knew these guys.

Then he seemed to shake himself. "So tell me, what do you want, Buddy? What do you really want out of baseball?"

What a weird question. I shrugged. "Gee, I don't know. I want to be a pro ballplayer someday, I guess. Doesn't everybody?"

"No, I mean right now. What do you want most in the world?"

He stared at me. His burning gaze made me nervous. I guess that's why I suddenly blurted out the truth.

"I—I want to play on a *good* team for once. No— it's more than that. I want to play on the best Shadyside team ever!"

Ernie nodded slowly. Without another word he turned and walked back to his house. He opened the door to go inside.

He suddenly turned around. "I guessed that might be your wish," he said. "Who knows? Maybe it will come true."

A smile crossed his lips. He started to chuckle.

Then he ducked inside.

"What's so funny?" I called through the screen door.

Ernie didn't answer.

I waited there for a minute. But he never returned.

"Weird," I muttered to myself. I glanced around the mess of a yard. Might as well leave.

I peeked through the hole in the fence. Eve was long gone.

The shortest way home was down Fear Street, so I walked around to the front of Ernie's house. And bumped right into a policeman. The officer clapped a hand on my shoulder. "Are you all right?" he asked me.

"I'm fine," I answered, startled. "Is something wrong?"

Eve ran up behind him. "I called the police, Buddy."

"You what? Why'd you do that?" I demanded. Eve was sort of a scaredy-cat. But calling the cops? That was ridiculous.

"I saw that weird old man grab you when you were under the porch," Eve explained. "I thought you were in trouble."

Another voice called behind me, "I checked it out. There's no sign of anyone. The house is empty, just like it should be."

I turned and saw another policeman walking down

the front steps. He looked older than the first officer, maybe in his fifties.

"What do you mean?" I asked. "Some old guy lives there."

"I don't think so, son," the first officer told me. "This house is abandoned."

What? The place *was* shabby, but abandoned?

I turned and stared up at the old house.

Whoa!

Cream-colored paint hung down in long curls from warped old boards. The shutters dangled crookedly from rusty hinges. All the windows were boarded up. Ivy grew thickly over the whole thing.

"But—I don't get it. I just met the guy who lives here," I said.

"Not possible," the older police officer told me. "No one has lived here since 1948!"

5

Two days later we played the Oneiga Blue Devils. By the fourth inning we were behind five to one. It was another runaway. As usual, I had the only run on the team.

"I'm telling you, that old man was a ghost!" Eve insisted.

She sat beside me in the dugout, munching sunflower seeds. She thought it made her look like a pro. I hated to break it to her. But she looked about as much like a pro as my cat, Foster.

"Come on, Buddy," Eve continued. "Fear Street? An abandoned house? A disappearing old man? Hello? You figure it out."

"Would you get off it?" I snapped. "That was two days ago. And besides, we're playing a *game* here, remember? Maybe you should pay more attention to that."

"Whoa. What's your problem?" She spat out the shell of a sunflower seed.

I frowned. I shouldn't have yelled at her like that. "Sorry," I mumbled. "I just can't stand losing—again."

Inside, I knew that wasn't the only reason I yelled. Really, I didn't want to think about the whole Fear Street thing. I mean, what if Eve were right? What if that old guy *was* a ghost?

Not that I really believed in that stuff. But still . . .

It was a relief when I noticed that I was next at bat.

"Gotta go," I said. "I'm on deck." I trotted to the on-deck circle, grabbed a bat, and swung it around to loosen up.

My teammate Scott Adams stood at first. He made it there on an error. Glen Brody was up at the plate. Maybe we could actually get some runs this inning.

Seeing Scott and Glen reminded me again of Fear Street. Scott lived there. Glen went over to his house all the time. Nothing weird ever happened to them.

Or did it? I remembered Glen telling some wild story at school once. Something about a monster from Fear Lake—

I stopped thinking about it when Glen popped the ball up into short left field.

"Run!" I shouted.

The Oneiga shortstop ran back for the ball, but

21

he collided with the left fielder. Scott was already rounding second base. Heading for third. Glen made it to first and then chugged toward second.

Safe!

Two runners in scoring position. All right! I told myself. Time to show these suckers a little something.

I felt pumped up as I approached the plate. My teammates cheered me on from the dugout. "Do it, Buddy!" "Go for it, Buddy!"

I stepped into the batter's box, ready to send this sucker downtown. Over the fence. Never to be seen again.

I grinned at the pitcher and waggled my bat a few times over the plate. He wiped some sweat from his brow.

Getting nervous? I taunted the pitcher in my mind. You better be. I'm going to mail this ball to Mars!

The first pitch was way outside. I let it go and moved closer to the plate, crowding it.

"Try to give me an outside pitch now, chicken," I muttered.

The pitcher wound up again. I tightened my grip on the bat.

Then, from the corner of my eye, I glimpsed a familiar face.

Ernie Ames. The old man from the house on Fear Street.

He stood at the fence. Watching me.

His eyes burned into mine. I felt as if I couldn't tear my gaze away from him.

What did he want?

"Duck!" someone yelled.

My head whipped around. Oh, man!

The ball was speeding straight toward me!

Whack! The ball hit me and knocked me down. My head smacked into the ground.

Even though I was wearing a helmet, pain exploded in my head. I saw a huge flash of white light. Little stars danced in front of my eyes.

Then everything went black.

6

The next thing I heard was somebody calling my name.

"Buddy. Buddy, talk to me," someone called.

I opened my eyes slowly. Man, did my head hurt!

My vision was blurry for a second. As it cleared, I made out faces peering down at me. Strangers.

"You okay, Buddy? That pitch hit you square in the head."

The man speaking was tall. And he had dark hair he wore slicked back with some sort of shiny oil.

How does he know my name? I wondered. I've never seen him before.

"Oooh!" I groaned and sat up slowly. My head throbbed where the ball hit me. I felt a little dizzy.

"Thatta boy. Can you get up?"

Without waiting for an answer, the shiny-haired man grabbed my arms and hauled me to my feet. I stood, wobbling for a second.

"Feeling steadier? Good. Shake it off," the man told me.

Shake it off? I thought. Is he crazy? I just got clobbered in the head with a fastball!

"I—uh—" I started to say.

"Hit by the pitch—take your base!" the umpire yelled.

"But I—"

"Come on, tough guy!" the man with the slicked-back hair interrupted. "You heard the ump. Go take your base." He tucked his hand under my elbow and hustled me to first base. "Good, good," he muttered, and trotted away.

Who was that guy anyway?

I stood at first base and squeezed my eyes shut, trying to get over my feeling of confusion.

"Batter up!" the umpire called.

I opened my eyes to see who was next at bat.

Whoa. Hold up, I thought. Who is *that* guy? He doesn't play on my team! And what's with his uniform?

The pants were baggy. The shirt was loose. The whole outfit looked like a sack. And instead of the red, white, and blue colors of my Shadyside Middle School uniform, it was white with black pinstripes.

Come to think of it, my own uniform felt strangely heavy and loose. I glanced down.

Black and white pinstripes! I was wearing pinstripes! How did that happen? Where was *my* uniform?

Before I could think, the batter hit a grounder toward the shortstop. I took off from first base. The ball skipped past the shortstop and into the outfield.

I rounded second at full speed, really running now. I slid into the bag and barely beat the throw to third.

I stood and brushed myself off. A rough hand clapped me on the shoulder.

"Way to hustle, Gibson," a deep voice said in my ear.

Gibson? Who was Gibson? I turned—and found myself staring at a man with a heavy red face.

He had to be the third-base coach—why else would he be standing there? But he wasn't *my* third-base coach. In fact, I'd never seen *this* guy before either.

What was happening? Who were these people? Was I seeing things because of my knock on the head? Was I going nuts?

I started to get a really weird feeling. . . .

I licked my lips. "Sanders," I corrected him. "My name is Sanders. Uh—who are you?"

The man laughed. "That's our Buddy. Always kidding around."

"Quit gabbing and get your head in the game," the man with the shiny hair called from across the field.

He had to be the head coach. But why didn't I recognize him?

I peered at the next batter—*another* person I didn't know. In fact, I couldn't find a single familiar face on the whole field—or in either of the dugouts. Eve, Scott, Glen—they had all disappeared!

It was the same with the people in the bleachers. Total strangers, all of them. And they all wore funny clothes. For example, there wasn't a woman there without a funny-looking hat on. And they all wore gloves. In the middle of the summer!

And where were my parents? They had been in the stands five minutes ago. But now I couldn't spot them anywhere.

The pitcher zoomed a fastball down the center of the plate. The guy at bat took a huge cut at it. He crushed the ball, sending it sailing out of the park.

"Home run!" people screamed.

"What's the matter with you, Gibson? Don't just stand there. Run home," the third-base coach urged.

I ran to home plate. Then I trotted to the dugout. As I passed the fence, I caught a glimpse of the parking lot.

Whoa. A huge maroon car with an odd, rounded shape sat next to a pickup truck. The car looked as if it came from one of those old gangster movies. The truck was straight out of the *Beverly Hillbillies* reruns I sometimes watch.

"Uh—are we sharing the park with a classic car

show today?" I asked a freckle-faced kid in the dugout.

He stared at me as if I were crazy.

"What's a classic car?" he asked.

I started to feel more than weird. I started to feel downright scared.

I could think of only one explanation for all this.

I *was* crazy. The knock on the head had made me go insane.

My temples throbbed. I sat on the bench and rubbed my head. My hair felt funny somehow. Stiff.

"Are you okay, Buddy? You don't look so hot," the freckle-faced kid told me.

I'm not okay! I wanted to shout. I'm going nuts!

But I was scared to say it out loud. What would they do to me if I were crazy? Take me off to a nuthouse?

"Head hurts," I mumbled at last.

I glanced down to the end of the dugout. A dozen strange, small gloves lay in a pile on the ground. They looked like pot holders. Leather pot holders. Not baseball mitts.

Nearby was a stack of wooden bats.

Wooden bats? Our league always used aluminum bats. Didn't we?

I was still trying to figure it all out, when the freckled kid poked me with a bat. "Get up, Buddy. Three outs."

"What?" I glanced up. Players in pin-striped uniforms streamed past me to the pile of gloves. It was our turn in the field.

I must have looked uncertain, because the man with the slicked-back hair reached into the pile and pulled out a glove.

"Get out there, Gibson," he barked. "We don't have all day."

I caught the glove and pulled it on as I ran for third. It looked small on my hand, but it felt like a perfect fit. Someone had written "Gibson" on it in blue ink.

That name again. I knew it from somewhere, but where?

Then, suddenly, I remembered the old man from yesterday. Ernie Ames. The guy Eve thought was a ghost.

Gibson was the kid Ernie told me about. Buddy Gibson. The kid in the photograph.

The photograph from *1948*.

I stopped running and stood there with my mouth open.

Could it be? Was it even possible?

I suddenly began to have trouble breathing. There was something I had to check out. Right away.

I dashed off the field and into the parking lot. I ran to the big maroon car and peered into the sideview mirror.

A stranger stared back out at me.

A stranger who had a blond crew cut instead of curly brown hair. Who had blue eyes, not brown. Who had a small scar over his right eyebrow. Who was about four inches taller than me.

A stranger who looked just like the kid in that 1948 photo.

The world seemed to swoop in a dizzy circle around me.

Now it was all starting to make sense—in a horrible way.

Now I understood why all the uniforms looked so goofy. Why the gloves were weird. Why everything seemed as if it had come from an antique shop.

And why everyone kept calling me Gibson.

Somehow, I *was* Gibson.

Somehow, I had gone back in time!

7

I stood there, stunned.

I had gone back in time!

Back—into someone else's body!

How? How did it happen?

I was broken out of my daze by the coach with the slicked-back hair. He ran over to me and grabbed my arm. "What is the matter with you, Gibson? Are you nuts?" he demanded. "Get out on that field. Now!"

He hustled me back to the diamond. I stumbled toward third base.

Think, I told myself. I just have to think.

"Hey, what inning is it?" I asked the catcher as I passed home plate.

"The ninth." He grinned. "Looks like another winner!"

I couldn't concentrate on the game at all. My mind kept whirling, trying to figure out what had happened. And how.

I rubbed the side of my head through my cap. There was still a little pain.

Was that it? I wondered. Could my knock on the head have made me *believe* I went back in time? Could it have made me see Buddy Gibson's face in the mirror instead of mine?

I nearly blew an easy play, when a line drive popped out of my tiny glove. But I scrambled to pick it up and managed to make the throw to first in time.

The left fielder hollered at me. "What's the matter, Gibson? Can't handle a little pepper?"

I glared back at him. He was tremendous—he looked closer to fourteen than twelve. He had reddish hair and a mean squint. I thought he might make a better linebacker than a fielder.

Normally, I would have answered him. But I kept my mouth shut. I didn't want to talk to anyone until I was sure of what was going on.

"Play ball!" the umpire shouted.

As the inning went on, I studied the people around me. Under their ball caps, most of the guys wore buzz cuts.

Most of *my* teammates, back in real time, had longer hair.

And my shoes. They were heavy, clunky, spiked things, stiff as iron. Nothing like my Nikes.

I *must* have gone back in time. Everything seemed so real. The nerdy-looking uniforms. The gloves.

Even the name "Gibson" written on my glove. The "S" was a little lopsided by the glove's seam. I couldn't *imagine* things in so much detail—could I?

I thought about Ernie. I played back our conversation in my mind, trying to remember everything he said about Gibson. And about 1948.

He said they called this team the Doom Squad. Because everyone that played them was doomed to lose.

And because—

I caught my breath, remembering the old man's words. "Now they're buried in the Fear Street Cemetery!"

They all died after the championship game!

I sucked in my breath. Holy cow! Was *this* the championship game?

I peered over my shoulder at the scoreboard in right field.

Shadyside, seven. Oneiga, two. We were up five runs in the ninth inning.

Ernie told me that in the championship game Shadyside was ahead by only two in the ninth.

Whew! It must be a different game. I was safe—for now.

But I had to get out of here before that game!

Then my mind flashed to another part of my

conversation with Ernie. My wish. I told him I wanted to play on the best Shadyside team ever.

Was that it?

Was my wish coming true?

"Strike three. You're out!" the umpire bellowed.

Three outs. The game was over. We won.

But it wasn't a victory I could enjoy.

As we were jogging in, the big left fielder pumped a fist in the air. "That's what you get when you play the Doom Squad, boys. A big 'L' in the score book. We are your doom!"

Doom. I shuddered at the word.

I *really* had to get out of here!

Then I thought of something. If I landed in the past because of a wish, maybe a wish would get me back to my own time!

I had to try. Outside the dugout, I tossed my glove down and shut my eyes tight. I balled my hands into fists.

I want to go home! I screamed in my mind. I want to go home!

"Okay, boys. Gather 'round," a voice called.

I opened one eye. Then the other.

The first thing I saw was the coach with the slicked-back hair.

I groaned. It was still 1948.

Everyone on the team gathered around. I joined them.

The coach stood with his hands in his jacket pockets. A cigarette dangled from his lips. Gross.

"Okay, guys, good job today," the coach said. "Keep playing like this, and we're on our way to the trophy for sure. We're just one game away. We'll be the champions of 1948! Let's hear it!"

"Yeah!" everybody cheered. Guys pounded me on the back.

I just stood there and tried to smile.

The players gathered their stuff. We crossed the parking lot to the bus. Everybody chattered away, laughing and happy.

Except me. I was miserable.

How was I going to get back to my own time?

I stood in line, waiting to board the bus. When I climbed the steps, I stopped in shock.

Behind the steering wheel sat the old man from the house on Fear Street! Ernie Ames!

He was here with me in the past!

My heart jumped in my chest.

If he made it to the past—maybe he could bring me back to the future.

Maybe.

8

"It's you!" I cried. I lunged at Ernie and grabbed him by the collar of his jacket. "I didn't mean it. Take me back. Take me back home. I don't want to be stuck here! Please!"

"Well, if you get out of everybody's way and let go of me, I'll be happy to take you back." The old man gave me a friendly smile.

"Really?" I gasped. "You will?"

Ernie laughed. "I'm the bus driver, Buddy. That's my job."

"No, I mean send me to the future. You can do it—can't you?"

Ernie's smile faded. I saw him shift his gaze to someone behind me.

The coach clapped a hand on my shoulder.

"Buddy took a knock today, Ernie," he told the bus driver. He pointed to his head. "Fastball right to the old noggin."

The bus driver nodded knowingly.

"Come on, Buddy. This way," the coach ordered, steering me away from the driver. He frowned down at me. "Maybe we better have a doctor check you out when we get home."

I grasped the coach's arm. "Please, you have to believe me! I'm not Buddy Gibson!"

The coach's frown deepened.

"I'm not!" I insisted. "I'm Buddy *Sanders*. And I'm from the future. I live in 1997!"

"Oh! So that's what this is." Coach grinned at me. "Sure, Buddy. You're from the future. And I'm the Lone Ranger. I'm just riding this bus until Silver comes along. He's my wonder horse, you know."

Laughter rang out all around me. Everyone on the team cracked up like this was some kind of joke.

I sighed, realizing the truth. No one believed me.

I turned and let the coach lead me to a seat. Why *should* they believe me? I thought. I sound completely crazy.

Coach stopped at a seat and pointed. "There you go, Buddy. And there's your book, right where you left it."

I glanced down. A novel lay on the seat. *Tom Swift and the Amazing Time Machine.*

"You and your science fiction," Coach grumbled. "I

don't know why you like that stuff so much. It'll rot your brain."

He picked up the book and leafed through the pages. "Where were you from last week? Mars, right?"

A short, sandy-haired kid with big buck teeth plopped into the seat next to me. "Yeah," he said. "Buddy was John Carter from Mars." He laughed.

The coach scanned the rows of seats. Then he walked up to the front. "Okay, Ernie. Everyone's here. Let's head out."

The bus jerked into motion. We pulled away from the Oneiga ball field.

"That Buddy's got some imagination," I heard the coach say to Ernie, the driver. "What a joker!"

This was awful. Not only did no one believe me—they didn't even think I was acting unusual. This Gibson kid made things up all the time.

We made a left turn at the end of the street and pulled onto a two-lane road. I stared out the window—we should be getting on the interstate! A six-lane highway! What happened to it?

I slouched back in my seat. It's 1948, I reminded myself. The interstate isn't even built yet.

Two seats in front of me, the big, ugly left fielder stood up. "Hey, guys, check this out," he called.

He pointed his arms straight out in front of him. "I am Buddy Gibson," he said in a robot voice. "I am from the future."

The kids sitting around him burst out laughing.

I glanced at the kid next to me. His face was covered with dark freckles. His big buck teeth stuck out even farther when he grinned at the fielder's joke. But at least he didn't laugh.

"What's your name?" I asked him.

"Don't play with me, Buddy. You've only known me your whole life." Then he frowned. "Say, how hard did that ball hit you?"

"Pretty hard," I told him. I leaned over and whispered, "I think maybe I have a little—what do you call it? Oh, yeah, amnesia."

The kid's eyes widened and he grinned. "Whoa! No kidding? That's neato!"

Neato?

Nerd-o! I thought.

"So—who are you?" I asked again.

"Johnny Beans. Center field. Remember?"

"Oh, yeah. Now I remember," I said. I wasn't lying. I *did* remember the kid—from the photograph the old man on Fear Street showed me.

"Who's the big doofus?" I pointed to the left fielder.

"That's Boog. Boog Johnson."

"He doesn't like me much, does he?" I asked.

"No, I guess he doesn't," Johnny agreed. "In fact, he doesn't like you—period."

Boog turned in his seat. He smirked at me. "Hey,

39

what's the news, future man? Who's going to win the World Series this year?"

Actually, I knew the answer to that. It was in one of my baseball books. The Cleveland Indians won in 1948. They beat Boston.

But I wasn't going to tell this jerk about it!

Boog stretched out his arms to either side. He ran up and down the aisle of the bus. "Get me. I'm Gibson in my very own space rocket. Zoom! Zoom!"

"Knock it off back there," the coach yelled. "No running around on the bus!"

Boog slinked back to his seat. He shot me a dirty look—as if it were my fault he got in trouble.

Turning my shoulder to Boog, I asked Johnny some more questions. He identified everyone on the bus for me. I sat back and pretended that it was all coming back to me.

As Johnny talked, I stared hard at the back of Ernie's head. Did he recognize me? Did he remember our meeting on Fear Street? I couldn't tell.

But he had to be the key to why I was here.

Maybe he did know who I was, but he didn't want to say so in front of all these people.

I had to find a way to talk to him when no one else was around.

I stared out the window, watching trees and buildings whiz by. Yes, I decided. That was—

I suddenly heard the sound of squealing brakes.

40

The bus shuddered to a stop. I pitched forward, banging my chin on the seat in front of me.

"Oof!" "Ow!" "Hey, watch it!" I heard my teammates holler.

"Sorry, guys," Ernie called back to us. "That truck in front of us skidded. We almost slammed into it. It was pretty close, but we're okay."

The accident! I thought. Sure, we're okay now. But soon a big old train really *will* slam into this bus! And if I don't do something, I'll be *in* the bus when it does!

No way. I had to get back to my own time before the train wreck happened. Before the championship game.

I turned to Johnny Beans.

"Tell me again. How many more games before the championship?"

Beans grinned. "Just one. Then we take the championship—and the trophy will be ours. Best in the state!"

It sounded great. But I knew the truth.

The Shadyside team wasn't going to win the championship game. They were doomed.

And if I didn't think of something fast—so was I!

9

The bus pulled into town on Village Road. I stared out the window. Would I recognize Shadyside in 1948?

We passed the fire department. And the police station. They both seemed pretty much the same.

But when I looked to my left, my mouth dropped open. Division Street Mall was gone! Or I guess it wasn't there yet. Neither was the ten-plex movie theater. Dalby's Department Store stood all by itself on the corner.

Across the street, the bowling alley stood as always, but a sign hung from it saying GRAND OPENING. Where the Rollerblading rink should have been, there was only an empty lot.

The bus continued along Village Road until we

reached the parking lot of Shadyside Middle School. I recognized the red brick building, even though the sign said SHADYSIDE JUNIOR HIGH SCHOOL.

Coach stood up at the front of the bus. "Okay, boys. We have one game before the championship. And I don't just want to beat this last team. I want to *destroy* them!"

"Yeah!" everybody yelled.

"I want them shaking in their shoes when we run out on that field!"

"Yeah!" the team replied.

"And why?"

"Because we're the Doom Squad!" the team roared.

"You bet we are." Coach nodded, looking satisfied.

Wow. My coach—my *real* coach, back in 1997— never talked like that. He said stuff like "Just remember, we're all out here to have fun."

Weird.

Coach put a hand on my arm as I was climbing off the bus. "How's the head, Buddy?" he asked. "Feeling better?"

"Yeah, Coach. I'm fine." I answered quickly.

I didn't want anyone to send me to a doctor. Who knows what medicine was like in 1948? What if they still used leeches to suck your blood or something?

"Glad to hear it," Coach said, smiling. "We can't afford to lose you. We might manage with somebody else hurt, but you're the star. We need you."

Out of the corner of my eye I saw Boog Johnson glaring at me. What was his problem?

As he walked past me, he leaned close to my ear and growled, "You think you're so hot."

"Forget him. He's just jealous," Johnny Beans whispered.

"I'd like to forget him, but I think he's going to pound me!" I said, worried.

"He wishes. I don't think he'd dare. Not until after the season anyway. His dad would kill him."

I started to walk toward my house on Spring Street. Then I remembered.

In 1948 I didn't live on Spring Street.

I wasn't even born yet.

My *parents* weren't even born yet!

I turned back to Johnny Beans. "Uh, I forgot where I live," I mumbled.

He shook his head. "Jeez, Louise, you *do* have amnesia!"

Jeez Louise? Man, these guys talked weird.

"Don't you remember?" Johnny continued. "Your house used to be in North Hills, but your folks moved last month. Now you're staying with Coach Johnson until the season's over."

"Oh—thanks," I said.

"Let's go, Gibson," someone shouted.

I turned and saw Coach standing by a humongous blue car. He waved at me. Boog stood next to him.

"Get a move on. I'm hungry," Boog bellowed.

I trotted over. Coach must be giving Boog a ride home.

Boog opened the front door.

"You get in back, son," the coach ordered. "Let Buddy ride up front with me."

Son?

That's when it hit me. Boog *Johnson?* Coach *Johnson?*

I groaned. I couldn't believe it! I was staying at the coach's house—that meant I was staying with Boog. The kid who wanted to pound me.

Great. Just great.

I climbed in and tried not to notice the stare Boog gave me.

I tugged hard on the heavy door to get it shut. Then I settled into the seat. Whoa! The coach's car was built like a tank!

Whoops! Have to buckle up, I thought. I dug around in the seat cushions.

"What are you doing?" Coach Johnson asked.

"I'm looking for my seat belt."

"Seat belt? What's a seat belt?" Boog scowled at me from the back.

Uh-oh . . . 1948 again. Maybe they didn't have seat belts in those days! "Heh-heh. Just joking," I mumbled.

"Seat belts," the coach snorted. "I've read about

them. Death traps, that's what they are. No, sir. I'm not letting anybody strap *me* into a car so I can't get away."

We drove out of the school parking lot and headed down Hawthorne Drive. We made a right turn on Park.

Then the coach turned right again—on Fear Street.

I should have guessed that's where Boog would live.

We cruised up the street, then turned left into the drive of a rambling two-story house. I got out of the car and glanced across the street.

A familiar-looking house stared back at me. Then I realized how I knew it. It was the house from my own time. The house where I met Ernie Ames, the bus driver.

The house where everything started.

Only now it didn't look abandoned. It was a little shabby, maybe, but the paint wasn't peeling off or anything.

An old car pulled into the house's driveway. The engine died and the bus driver stepped out.

He waved to me. I waved back slowly.

Did he recognize me? I mean *me,* Buddy Sanders?

I've got to talk to him, I thought. Alone. I need to find out why he sent me here—and how I'm supposed to get back to my own time.

"Buddy," Coach Johnson called. "Come on inside."

"Sure," I said. I walked slowly toward the Johnsons' house.

Everything is going to be okay, I told myself. All I have to do is stay calm.

Calm—hah! If I knew then what was about to happen to me, I would have run screaming down Fear Street.

Because my nightmare was just starting!

10

We tromped up the wooden steps to the front door. A lady who had to be Boog's mom stood in the doorway, waiting for us.

Her red hair hung to her shoulders, and her cheeks had a rosy glow. She wore a dark blue dress with a white lace collar.

"Don't take another step without taking those muddy shoes off! I just scrubbed these floors," she scolded. Then she smiled. "So, how did we do today, boys?"

"A feast for your conquering heroes!" Coach Johnson teased.

Mrs. Johnson laughed. "I guess you won again."

"Don't we always, Mom?" Boog asked.

"It was a close call though," the coach said. "We almost lost our star player to a fastball to his head."

Mrs. Johnson gasped. "Oh, no! Here, Buddy, let me see." She tipped my head to the side and probed gently at the bruise. She made a soft "tsk."

"It looks painful," she told me. "But I think you'll live. Not a lot of swelling. Any dizziness, Buddy? Are you feeling sleepy?"

"I'm okay," I mumbled.

"Good. Now, you boys run upstairs and wash up for supper. Everything's ready. Go on, scoot."

I followed Boog up the stairs, thinking that people were sure a lot less careful in 1948. In my own time, Mom and Dad would have sent me to the doctor as soon as I was hit.

I stopped at the top of the stairs and looked around, confused. Boog stood in a doorway. "Well? You just going to stand there?" he snapped.

"I don't remember—"

Boog's eyes narrowed. "What's with you, Buddy?" He pointed to a door down the hall. "In there. I got dibs on the bathroom."

He stepped into the bathroom and slammed the door. I heard water running. Good. He was out of my way. Now I could really check the place out.

I went down the hall and opened the door to the room Buddy Gibson was staying in. It was smaller than the one I had at home, but it looked nice and cozy. It had a shelf filled with Hardy Boys and Tarzan books. Hey! I read those—way in the future. Gibson had a few of those Tom Swift books too.

I looked around for the stereo. It was nowhere to be found.

Maybe he's got a TV, I thought. But I couldn't find one of those either.

Duh—1948. Hardly anyone had TVs back then.

So what did people do for fun around here?

I spied a window at the far end of the room. I walked over to it and lifted the blinds.

Yes! The window faced the front. I could see Fear Street, and Ernie the bus driver's house.

I glanced down. A rose trellis clung to the side of the house—right below the window. Perfect for climbing out after dark. All right!

Someone knocked on the door. I dropped the blinds.

"I'm done in the bathroom. You're up, goofus," Boog bellowed from the other side.

"Keep your shirt on, you big loser," I muttered under my breath.

There was a chest of drawers positioned against the wall behind me. A mirror was placed over it.

I stooped to open one of the drawers, and caught my reflection in the mirror. There it was again. Buddy Gibson's face, with the blue eyes and the scar. I shuddered.

Looking like someone else—*being* someone else—

was the creepiest part about this whole nightmare. A guy just doesn't expect to see someone else in the mirror.

I opened one of the dresser drawers. Inside I found shirts and pants, neatly folded and sorted. The shirts were all plaid. That wouldn't have been so bad if they were flannel. But they weren't. They were this scratchy cotton material. They had short sleeves and narrow collars.

The pants were mostly jeans. Stiff, dark blue jeans that looked like they could stand up all by themselves.

I changed into fresh clothes, then glanced in the mirror again. Geek city! I wouldn't be caught dead in these clothes back home.

But this was 1948. I'd probably blend right in with all the other nerds here.

The door opened again, and Boog came in. "Come on, supper's waiting." He jabbed at me with his fist. I jerked backward.

"Hah! Flinch!" he said, and grabbed my arm. "Frog!" Then he hit me hard in the muscle of my left arm.

"Ow!" I cried. "Hey, that hurt." I made a fist.

When Boog saw it, his lips curled in a mean smile.

"You flinched, tough guy," he reminded me. "So I get to frog you. That's the rule, and you know it. Or are you too big a sissy to trade licks?"

He sneered and pushed me backward. "Huh?" he challenged. He shoved me again. "How about it? You

51

too much of a baby? Or maybe you want to go outside and fight for real?" He shoved me again.

I had just about had enough of this guy. He was big. But I didn't care. Nobody pushes me around like that.

"Quit it!" I shouted. I shoved him back—hard— and caught him by surprise. He stumbled backward and tripped on the rug. He landed with a crash. Right on his rear end.

He picked himself up. "Now you're going to get it!" he snarled.

I'd studied karate for two months when I was eleven. I took a stance, just like my instructor showed me.

Boog didn't know it, but I was about to become the Karate Kid.

Then Boog stood up to his full height.

Uh-oh, I thought. He's really big, isn't he?

And he looks really strong.

Boog came at me with his fist cocked back.

Yikes! I thought. Here it comes!

And then he swung—straight at my face.

Boog's fist drove toward my face.

I gritted my teeth.

Then Coach Johnson's voice roared up the stairs.

"Knock off the roughhousing, you two. You sound like a herd of elephants up there!"

Boog's fist stopped—an inch from my nose. He grinned at me.

"You got lucky, Gibson. But next time I'm going to pulverize you."

"Yeah, sure," I said. I rubbed the sore place on my arm and glared at him. No way would I let him know I was scared.

But I was.

Boog went out of the room first. I stayed behind a second to calm down. And think.

Being trapped in the past was bad enough. But now I had another problem. Boog.

I had to get out of there before he pulverized me.

I had to talk to Ernie. Tonight!

Dinner was incredible. Thick slabs of roast beef. Gravy. Mashed potatoes. Peas glistening with butter. Creamed corn. Slices of white bread smeared with *more* butter. Peach cobbler with cream for dessert.

My mom cooks "heart-healthy" food. I think she would have fainted at the sight of all that fat.

It tasted great. But by the time I worked through my second helping of cobbler, I was worried that I might burst.

Did they eat like this every day?

After dinner everyone sat in the living room and listened to the radio. Some guy named Fred Allen. The Johnsons all thought he was a riot. I couldn't figure out what was so funny myself. Another thing that changed since 1948, I guess.

I sat around with them as long as I could stand it. Then I stood up and stretched. "I think I'll go to bed," I announced.

Boog curled his lip. "What are you, a baby? It's only a quarter to nine."

"Buddy needs his rest," Coach Johnson snapped. "Especially after that knock on the head. You go along, Buddy."

I didn't miss the dirty look Boog shot me.

54

I wished his dad had kept quiet. He was trying to help, I guess. But really, he made Boog hate me even more.

I trudged up the stairs and into my room. Standing by the door, I listened for a moment. Good. They were all still laughing away at Fred Allen.

Time to pay a visit to the bus driver.

The window in my room was already open wide. I swung my legs over the sill. Then I let myself down until I dangled by my hands. I grasped the wooden rose trellis and began to climb.

"Ow. Ouch!" I muttered under my breath. Thorns pricked through my plaid shirt and into my skin.

When I reached the bottom, I crept across the lawn to the Johnsons' hedge. I peered over its leafy top at the bus driver's house.

The lights on the first floor were still on. They cast a faint light over his overgrown lawn. It was a good thing, because all the streetlamps on the block were out.

Just one more cheerful detail about Fear Street.

I stole across Fear Street. I made my way up to the bus driver's rickety porch. I climbed up to the door and knocked softly.

Ernie opened the door. "Buddy! What are you doing here?" He smiled. "This is a nice surprise. I don't get a lot of visitors. Come on in."

He didn't have to ask me twice. I barreled past him into the house.

He closed the door. "Would you like a soda pop, or—"

"Listen," I interrupted. "I don't know why you sent me back here—or how. But this is not what I wished for—understand? I want to go home. You have to send me back!"

Ernie's eyebrows drew together. "Take it easy, Buddy. What are you talking about?"

"I know you remember me," I insisted. The words tumbled out of my mouth. "I'm Buddy *Sanders*—not Buddy Gibson. I'm from the future. You sent me here because of my wish. Because I wished to be on the best team ever. But I wanted *my* team to be the best team ever. I didn't want to be here!"

A strange look crossed Ernie's face. "All right, Buddy," he said in a soothing voice. "You want me to send you back? I'll send you back. No problem."

"You—you will?" I stared at him. I didn't think it would be so easy.

"Just wait right there," Ernie instructed. "I—uh— I have to get the time machine ready." He shuffled out of the room, pulling the door closed behind him.

Time machine? I never thought of that. It never occurred to me that I was brought here by a machine. But I guessed it made sense. How else could Ernie move people back and forth?

Then in the other room I heard Ernie's voice. He spoke softly. Who was he talking to? I thought he lived alone.

I walked over to the door he went through. It was open a crack. His voice drifted through.

"Get me the Johnson house, Eunice. . . . Yeah, I know it's right across the street from me, but this is an emergency!"

Wait a minute. What was he doing?

"Hello, Mr. Johnson?" Ernie whispered. "I think you'd better come over here right away. Buddy's here." He paused. "How should I know how he got here? All I know is, he's here, and he's talking crazy. Saying he wants me to send him back to the future. And believe me—he's not kidding. That fastball did more damage than you think!"

Oh, no! I realized. Ernie thinks I'm *nuts!*

I had to get out of there—fast. Or they would stick me in some hospital for sure.

I didn't want to go to a hospital. I just wanted to get back home—to my own time.

I raced to Ernie's front door and threw it open.

Coach Johnson strode up the walk outside.

"No!" I gasped. I tore into Ernie's kitchen. I knew there was a back door in there—I remembered Ernie using it when I met him the first time.

There! I darted over and slid the bolt.

Then I ran into the night. Through Ernie's backyard. Around the side of his house. And down Fear Street—in the dark.

Coach Johnson's voice rang out behind me. "Buddy! Stop!"

57

I sprinted down the street. Heavy steps pounded after me.

I had no idea where I was going. I just ran.

Then, directly in front of me, I saw a patch of deeper darkness. It was just . . . black. Like the deepest shadow on a bright, sunny day.

It lay across my path. A wave of cold washed toward me.

The hair rose on the back of my neck.

I didn't even slow down. I just veered to my left. I ran toward a tall iron gate. Through it I glimpsed shadowy trees and a lot of whitish rocks. Maybe I could hide in there.

It wasn't until I passed through the gates that I began to guess where I was. The white rocks—why did they all have the same shape? Sort of rectangular, with rounded tops.

Uh-oh.

They weren't plain old rocks.

They were gravestones.

I was in the Fear Street Cemetery!

12

The Fear Street Cemetery!

My skin crawled. I wasn't about to hide in *there*. I had to find a way out!

I slowed to a jog, peering right and left.

"Buddy!" Coach Johnson called again. "Where are you going? Come back!"

His voice sounded close. I risked a glance over my shoulder.

The next thing I knew, I was flying through the air. I must have caught my foot on a root or something.

I whacked my head hard on a low branch.

Then I hit the ground.

And everything went black.

* * *

When I opened my eyes again, the first thing I saw was Mrs. Johnson's worried face. She bent over me, biting her lip.

I couldn't help groaning. And not just because my head was killing me.

I was right back where I started! At the Johnsons' house. In Buddy Gibson's bedroom.

Another face came into view. A silver-haired man with a white coat. He peered deep into my eyes as I lay in bed. "Can you hear me, son?"

"Yes," I mumbled.

"What's your name?" he asked.

"Buddy. My name is Buddy."

"What's your last name?" he wanted to know.

There was no point telling the truth. I already found that out. Nobody believed me.

I gritted my teeth. "Gibson," I replied.

"Good, good. And what year is this?"

"It's 1948," I muttered.

Then the doctor shined a light in my eyes and asked me to follow his finger as he moved it around. I did what I was told.

The doctor straightened up. "He's all right," he told Mrs. Johnson. "No sign of concussion. And he doesn't seem confused anymore. My guess is, that second knock on the head knocked his wits back into order." He laughed.

I glared at him from my bed. I didn't think it was funny at all.

"Keep an eye on him for the next few days, and let me know if you notice any more strange behavior," the doctor advised. "But I think he'll be just fine."

"Thank you, Doctor." Mrs. Johnson breathed a sigh of relief. The doctor left the room.

Mrs. Johnson leaned down and touched me on the forehead. "You gave everyone quite a scare, Buddy," she told me. Then she smiled. "But you're okay now. Try to get some rest."

"I'll try. Sorry for all the trouble, Mrs. Johnson," I said, closing my eyes.

She snapped off my lamp and went out. I lay there in the dark, thinking.

What went wrong with Ernie? He definitely didn't know what I was talking about. Did that mean he wasn't the one who brought me to the past?

Then I thought of an explanation that made my skin prickle.

There was a good reason Ernie didn't know what I was talking about. To him, the bus crash was still in the future. How could he know about something that hadn't happened yet?

That meant the Ernie that I met in my own time— the one who asked me what my wish was—really was a ghost. Eve was right.

I swallowed hard. So a ghost sent me into the past. But why? Why?

The question echoed in my brain until I finally fell asleep.

I don't know how much time went by. It felt like only a second passed before I was jerked awake. I lay in bed, listening.

What woke me?

I shivered. The room was strangely cold—even though it was the middle of summer. I gathered the sheet tighter around me.

I glanced at the alarm clock. With the moonlight from the window I could just make out the time. Three in the morning.

I swept my eyes around the room. Everything seemed normal, but the hairs on the back of my neck bristled. I had a feeling there was someone else there. Even though I could see no one.

A shadow moved across from me.

I sat up in bed. My heart thudded. "Boog? Is that you?" I demanded.

No answer.

"This isn't funny, man." I tried to keep my voice steady.

Still no answer. But the shadow seemed to drift in front of the window. The moonlight suddenly grew dimmer.

I strained my eyes in the darkness. All I could see was—black. Like the patch of inky shadow I saw on Fear Street earlier that night.

"Wh-who's there?" I stammered.

The darkness seemed to stretch toward me.

"You! Why did you do this to me?" a thin, cold voice whispered.

No way was that Boog's voice! Chills raced down my back.

"Who—who are you?" I croaked.

The shadow moved closer. It looked like a cloud of thick black smoke—with burning white holes for eyes!

Was it a ghost?

It loomed right in front of my face. "You'll pay!"

"Wh-what did I do? What do you want?" I managed to ask.

No answer. The shadow bulged toward me.

I shrank back. Numbing cold seeped into my bones.

Then the thing was on top of me. Covering my face. Pressing me down.

"Help!" I tried to shout. But I couldn't make a sound.

I couldn't breathe!

The shadow was crushing me!

13

I was being smothered—by a shadow!

I gasped and strained for air. Fingers of cold dug deep into my veins. It felt as though my blood was turning to ice.

I pushed against the shadow.

My hands passed right through it!

The horrible cold weight was crushing the air right out of my lungs. And I couldn't even touch it!

I grasped desperately at the thing. But my fingers closed on nothing.

This is it, I thought. I'm finished!

Then, suddenly, I could breathe again.

No more horrible weight on my chest.

No more icy chill.

I was struggling with my own sheets.

I peered around the room. My breath rasped loudly in the stillness. Moonlight poured in through the open window.

I lay there, shaking. Was it a dream? A horrible nightmare?

Then a ghostly voice whispered in my ear.

"I'll be back," it said. "I'm coming for you. And next time I'll be stronger."

I gasped. No dream. It was no dream!

A ghost attacked me!

A ghost from the Fear Street Cemetery.

Okay. I was ready to admit it.

"I believe in ghosts," I whispered.

But what did it want with me? What did *I* do to it? I didn't have a clue!

Gradually, the numbness bled from my veins. My breathing returned to normal.

My hand trembled as I flicked on the lamp. I swung my feet down to the floor and sat up. I glanced over at the mirror.

Buddy Gibson's square face stared back at me.

"Why?" I asked the reflection. "Why did you have to be living on Fear Street, of all places?"

Now things were even worse than before!

Not only did Boog want to pound me into the ground. Not only was I trapped in the past.

Now I had some crazy Fear Street ghost after me!

What was next? Plagues? Floods? Other natural disasters?

I remembered the ghost's words. It said it was getting stronger. And coming back.

What was I going to do?

There was only one answer. I had to get out of there before the thing came back.

But once again I had a basic problem: How?

Wishing didn't work. Neither did hitting my head again, the way I did in the cemetery. Not that I planned that!

And I knew now that Ernie wasn't going to help me. He didn't even know what I was talking about.

"Use your brain, Buddy," I told myself. "Think."

What did I know about time travel?

Not much! Until yesterday I never even believed it was possible.

I thought of all the TV shows I'd seen with time travel in them. In most cases, people traveled through time on purpose.

But then I remembered this one show where the guy couldn't control his travel. Like me.

In the show he could move on only if he changed history for the person whose body he was stuck in.

I thought about that. Change history.

Maybe *I* was supposed to change history!

But change *what?*

Then I slapped my forehead. Of course. The answer was obvious!

"The bus crash!" I said aloud.

Maybe I was supposed to save Gibson and his teammates from dying!

Maybe I was supposed to be a hero!

Cool.

But how could I do it?

Hmmm. Maybe if we lost our last game—tomorrow's game.

Yeah! I thought. That's it!

I paced around the room, excited. "If I throw the game—if I make Shadyside lose—the team won't make the championships," I whispered. "Then they won't be on that bus when the train comes by. Everyone would be saved!"

And maybe *I* would get to go back to my time.

The more I thought about it, the more it made sense. I was supposed to change history. That had to be it.

Okay. It was up to me to see we never played that championship game. One game to go, and all I had to do was make sure we lost it.

I hated the idea of throwing a game. Whenever I played baseball, I played to win. But really, what was more important—playing your best, or saving about twenty lives?

The answer was obvious. I knew what I had to do. Tomorrow the Shadyside team would be playing a crucial game.

And their big star, Buddy Gibson, would be doing his very best—to lose!

14

The next day was cloudy and muggy. I broke a sweat just getting out of bed. Why didn't someone turn on the air-conditioning?

Oh, yeah, 1948. No air-conditioning.

Still, the rotten weather had its good points. I lifted the blinds on the bedroom window and cheered on the clouds.

"Come on, guys. Rain us out," I whispered.

If we didn't play the game tonight, it would have to be played tomorrow. When we were supposed to be at the championships. History would change!

Then I remembered. In the past this game wasn't called because of rain. Shadyside played as scheduled. The weather was going to clear up—whether I liked it or not.

I sighed and went down to the kitchen. I began looking through the cabinets for some cereal or a Pop-Tart.

Mrs. Johnson pushed through the swinging doors from the dining room. "Buddy!" she cried. "How are you feeling?" She held me by the shoulders, studying my face. Her blue eyes were full of concern.

She was a nice lady. I felt bad for worrying her.

"I'm fine. Really," I answered. "Sorry I scared you yesterday. I—uh—I guess I was a little confused."

"Don't give it another thought, dear," Mrs. Johnson told me. "Go on into the dining room. Your breakfast is waiting."

I slid into a seat in the dining room. The table was covered with platters of pancakes, bacon, eggs, and potatoes. Boog sat there with a full plate, chowing down.

"Wow," I muttered under my breath. It was amazing to me these people could even move, they ate so much!

I loaded my plate with some pancakes and bacon. "Where's Coach?" I asked Boog.

He scowled at me. "At work, stupid."

While Boog and I ate, Mrs. Johnson fluttered around, dusting things. She wore a pink dress with a flowered apron tied over it.

I can't imagine *my* mom doing housework in a dress. She cleans in a grubby sweatshirt and a pair of old jeans.

I pushed my plate away and glanced at Boog. "What time is the game?" I asked.

"About three. Dad is leaving work early to make it there on time." He shoved one last giant forkful of eggs into his mouth and stood up. "Come on," he said. "Let's hit some flies and rollers."

"Okay," I agreed after a second.

I was surprised that Boog wanted to play ball with me. I hoped he wasn't just trying to get me alone so he could finish beating me up.

But I figured I might as well take the chance. It wasn't like I had anything else to do before the game.

The sun was already beaming through the clouds when we went outside. We crossed to Ernie's house and went through his backyard. Boog shoved aside the same fence boards I crawled through all those years in the future. We squirmed through the fence, into the same field where Eve and I practiced.

I mean, where we were *going* to practice, in fifty years.

Whatever. My brain was starting to hurt.

Boog's version of flies and rollers went like this: You catch five flies or ten ground balls to earn a turn at bat. Boog batted first, and man, did he make me work! He swatted balls all over the field. By the time I earned my chance at bat, I must have trotted two miles.

"Made you run," he snickered when he handed me the bat.

"Yeah, well, we'll see how you do, big guy," I puffed. I was so hot, I thought I might explode.

Boog hustled across the field, and I started hitting to him.

Anything I hit above his head, he could catch. No problem. But grounders and drives below the waist were hard for him.

After watching him for a minute, I waved him over. We ran and met about halfway.

"I think I know what you're doing wrong," I said.

Boog flushed. "Oh, yeah? I do all right, smart guy."

"Hey, chill out. I'm just trying to help."

"Chill out?" he sneered. "Where did you learn that dumb expression?"

"Uh, I—I heard it somewhere, I guess," I stammered. I had to watch what I said. *Chill out* was from way after Boog's time. "Anyway, I think I can help you with those low ones."

Boog folded his arms. "Is that so?"

Maybe this wasn't such a good idea, I thought. Boog was starting to look as if he wanted to pound me again. And anyway, the worse he played, the more chance we would have of losing the game today—and missing the championship.

"All right, genius, I'm waiting," Boog growled.

Me and my big mouth.

"See, it's natural to catch a high one," I began. "You put the glove between your eyes and the ball.

But for low ones, you put the glove between the ball and the ground, or the ball and your body. So you have to hold your head differently for those."

He looked slightly puzzled. "Yeah?"

"Yeah. Watch." I bent over and showed him what I meant, following the path of an imaginary ball.

He turned his glove, mimicking my moves.

Then, to my surprise, he grinned. "Hit me some."

He turned and chugged across the field. I trotted back to the fence and hit him a short fly ball, making him run up. He turned his glove at the last minute. The ball bounced off.

"Hold it like a basket for those," I yelled. "Open."

I hit him another. He got it that time. Then the next one, and the next, and the next.

By the time we finished, Boog was snagging everything I could hit. He ran up, grinning. "It works. Did you see that?" He pounded his fist in his glove. "Wait till Dad sees me now!"

I couldn't help grinning back at him. And it wasn't just because now he wouldn't try to beat me up anymore. It's corny, but I actually felt glad I helped Boog.

Boog pulled off his glove and shouldered the bat. "Come on, let's go see if Mom's got some lemonade."

We walked back to the fence. Boog crawled through. I glanced up and saw Ernie staring at us from an upstairs window.

72

The day suddenly seemed less bright. For a minute there, I had forgotten where I was. Playing ball, joking with Boog, made me relax.

But seeing Ernie reminded me of everything that happened the night before. The ghost, or whatever it was, that nearly smothered me in my bed.

I had to find a way to lose the game today. I had to get out of there *now*. If I didn't, it was going to take a lot more than lemonade to make me feel better.

Because that thing was coming back for me!

15

The game was played in Shadyside this time. No bus. We were the home team, so we took the field first. I stood at third and banged my fist into my glove. I was trying to beam mental messages to the batter.

Want to score some runs? I thought at him. Just hit it my way, and I'll see what I can do for you.

The first two batters struck out, but the third hit one my way I let it bounce off my glove. Then I chased after the ball as if I were in a hurry. I made sure I kicked it just as I reached to pick it up.

By the time I got the ball, the runner was on second. I decided to settle for that. If I made too many errors on one play, it would look suspicious.

"What is with you, Gibson?" Johnny Beans yelled. "You got holes in your glove or something?"

I shrugged my shoulders. "Sorry," I called back. I tried to sound as if I meant it.

The next batter walked. That meant the other team had runners on first and second, with two out.

The next batter kept fouling out to the left. I thought he might hit one down the third baseline, so I edged toward second.

Sure enough, he hit a bouncer right toward third base.

I made a big deal about diving for the ball. I knew I was short. It would go on by.

But then something weird happened.

The ball looked as if it struck an invisible wall in midair. It hung in the air for a split second.

Then it curved around and wobbled into my glove—without me doing a thing!

Huh?

I tried to miss it—but I caught it anyway!

"Nice play, Gibson!" Coach Johnson roared.

I climbed to my feet, staring at the ball in my glove.

The runner from second charged right into me for the third out.

The crowd in the bleachers cheered wildly as our team ran off the field. My teammates slapped me on the back and congratulated me. Even Boog called out, "Good one!"

"What a play!" Johnny Beans exclaimed as we tossed down our gloves. "How did you do that? I thought that ball was by you for sure!"

I shrugged. "Just a lucky break," I mumbled.

But it didn't *feel* like a lucky break. I was almost positive that ball changed course in midair.

Then a voice whispered behind me, "I know what you're doing, you rat. You're trying to lose! But I won't let you."

I whirled around.

No one behind me.

"Did—did you say something?" I asked Johnny.

"Nope," he replied.

But I knew that already.

Because I recognized that thin, cold voice. The voice from last night. From the ghost, or whatever it was, that attacked me.

It followed me! It was here!

And somehow it was interfering with the game!

Why? What did a ghost care about a baseball game? Why did a ghost want Shadyside to win?

In the dugout, I checked the lineup sheet. I was batting cleanup.

Good. I would make sure I struck out. There was nothing a ghost could do to prevent *that!*

The bases were loaded when I got to the plate. I stepped up with a hollow feeling in my stomach. I was never at bat before when I didn't try to do my best. But I made myself swing at the first two pitches like a goof.

My teammates yelled from the dugout.

"Use your eyes, Buddy."

"Don't swing at junk!"

"Come on, Gibson!"

I swung at the third pitch, a ball way outside. There was no way I could hit it.

Then the ball changed course.

Not like a curveball. It was as if the ball whacked into something and bounced off. It hit me on the elbow.

The umpire jumped up and hollered, "Hit by the pitch! Automatic walk. Take your base!"

I groaned and slung my bat toward the dugout. I trudged to first as the kid on third ambled home.

"Hah," the cold voice whispered in my ear. "You can't stop me. I'm growing stronger. I'm going to get you!"

I shuddered.

I was starting to realize the horrible truth.

I couldn't lose.

No matter what I did, the ghost wasn't going to let me throw the game. I didn't know why.

All I knew was, my chance to change history was going down the tubes.

And so was my chance to survive!

16

We won the game seven to three. Boog was a maniac in the outfield. He made one incredible play after another.

As for me, I kept trying my best to lose the game. But the harder I tried, the more I looked like a star.

My plays seemed impossible. The other guys started to stare at me as if I were some kind of wizard or something.

I couldn't blame them. The plays were totally impossible. The ghost made them all happen. I had nothing to do with it.

If I tripped over my own feet, something would make me sail gracefully through the air and snag a line drive like a Hall of Famer.

If I threw wide, the ball would curve like a Frisbee and smack solidly into the first baseman's glove.

If I hit a fly ball, it would just keep going—and going—until it soared over the fence and vanished.

I could have played standing on my head and never missed a lick.

It was horrible!

After the game, Coach Johnson drove Boog and me into town. He dropped us off at a little grocery store. "I've got to do some errands," he explained. "Why don't you boys get yourselves a few goodies? My treat." He reached into his pocket.

Excellent! I thought. I'd really love a can of soda right now. And maybe a candy bar.

Then coach handed each of us a quarter.

A quarter! I stared at the coin. What could I possibly get for twenty-five lousy cents?

"Thanks, Dad!" Boog said happily. "Let's go, Buddy."

I followed him into the tiny store. It was crammed with old-fashioned–looking cans and bottles, stacked on wooden shelves. Jars of hard candy lined the counter. Below them lay rows of candy bars and gum.

A big red cooler stood by the counter. COCA-COLA was written on the side. Boog walked over to it and opened the lid.

I peered inside and saw rows of bottles hanging from racks by their tops. Boog slid a Coke free. I watched closely and did what he did.

When I opened it, the drink was just a little bit frozen. It tasted really good. Even better than Coke usually tasted.

And the best part was, I bought the Coke, a bag of gum, and a Three Musketeers bar for only eleven cents! Also, the candy bar was definitely bigger than the ones in my own time.

I guess 1948 did have its good points.

Boog and I sat on a bench in front of the store. We ate our candy while we watched the cars go by.

Boog was obviously feeling good. "Did you hear what Dad told me?" he asked, trying to sound casual. "He said it was the best he'd ever seen me play."

"You had a great game," I agreed glumly.

"Not as good as yours though," Boog said generously. He drained his soda and belched. "I feel like I hit my stride today. I just wish the season wasn't almost over."

"I know. I wish it would go on too," I agreed.

Boy, did I wish!

But tomorrow was the championship. Do-or-die time.

No joke!

Boog leaned back on the bench and took a deep breath. "Just smell that summer air, Buddy. That's baseball air. And tomorrow will be the best day. We'll win the championship and everyone will know we're number one. Man, life is sweet."

His words made me feel miserable. The best day? Hardly. The *last* day was more like it. The *worst* day.

There had to be something more I could do to stop the accident!

I could run away, I thought. Then I could hide long enough to stay off that bus. To stay alive.

But what about everybody else on the team? What about Johnny Beans? And Boog?

Maybe I should try to tell Boog what I knew. Then he would know to stay off the bus too.

Forget it. He would just think I was crazy—like everyone else did. "Been there, done that," I muttered.

"What?" Boog asked.

"Nothing," I answered, sighing.

No. There was nothing I could do but run away. Save myself—and hope that I could find my way back to my own time someday. I couldn't worry about the rest of the team.

And then I got an idea.

It was so simple, I almost didn't believe it could work. But the more I thought about it, the more it made sense.

Yes!

A stupid grin crept across my face. "You know what?" I said.

"What?" Boog glanced at me.

"We *are* going to win that game tomorrow," I declared.

He laughed. "Sure we are!" He punched me on the shoulder. "We're the Doom Squad! We have to win!"

You are so right, I thought. We *have* to win!

If we win, we'll go to the party after the game. We won't get right on the bus to go home.

And we won't be on those tracks when the train comes to squash us.

And I know how to win the game! I know what the last play will be! Ernie told me about it before I ended up in the past.

All I have to do is hug the foul line and grab that last line drive. And I'll save the whole team!

I'll change history!

Butterflies fluttered in my stomach. Now that I knew what to do, I wondered if I could pull it off. Everything had to go just right. I had to play the best game of my life!

All I knew was, I'd *better* have what it takes.

Then I remembered my other little problem.

That ghost. It told me it was coming back. Coming for me.

Would I still be around for tomorrow's game?

17

That night, as I brushed my teeth in the bathroom, I got the feeling someone was watching me.

I stopped mid-brush. Toothpaste ran from my mouth. I glanced up into the mirror.

No one there.

After a second, I spat out the rest of the toothpaste and reached for the towel.

Wait—did I glimpse something in the mirror?

No. It was only me. Or, rather, Buddy Gibson. His face looked back at me from the mirror. It still freaked me out. That blond crew cut. The scar. They didn't belong to me!

Shivering, I turned away from the mirror. I went into my room and slid into bed. I switched off the lamp. Darkness surrounded me.

I listened to the sounds of the house settling down. I had to stay awake. I didn't want that ghost to catch me by surprise. Once I was sure the adults were in bed, I would switch the lamp back on.

But even though I was terrified, I was wiped out. After a while I drifted off.

When I opened my eyes again, it was hours later. I lay in bed, tense.

The last time I woke like this, I had a visitor.

I stared around. I saw nothing unusual.

Moonlight poured through the window. My desk chair cast a long shadow on the wall.

Very slowly I sat up, careful to make no sound. I studied the shadows.

Did this one move? Did that one?

"You're just working yourself up," I whispered.

But *something* woke me. I was sure of it.

And something was different about this room. What was it?

The closet door. It was closed. Wasn't it open when I went to bed?

Mrs. Johnson probably came in and shut it while I was asleep, I thought. That's all.

But I couldn't convince myself. The more I stared at the door, the more nervous I got.

I licked my lips. I felt my heart stepping up its rhythm. I had to do something before I scared myself to death.

I reached for the lamp switch and turned it.

The bulb blew out with a loud crackle.

"Great," I muttered. "Just great."

I eased out of bed and tiptoed to the door. I flipped the switch for the overhead light. I sighed with relief as light flooded the room.

The shadows vanished.

Now, with the light on, my fears felt foolish. Just my imagination running away with me. I took a deep breath, trying to calm my racing heart.

Now I could go back to bed.

Wait. Not just yet.

I had to see if there was anything behind the closet door.

I padded over to the closet and put my hand on the doorknob. I turned it.

CRACKKKKK!

The overhead bulb blew out.

I tried to slam the door shut. But it was too late. It swung open with a slow creak. I couldn't hold it closed.

I gasped. The moonlight fell across a figure in the closet. It was dark, smoky. It seemed wrapped in shadows. But this time I could make out features.

Human features. A head. A neck. A face.

I backed away from the closet. Cold sweat prickled on my forehead.

The ghost floated forward. Its arms rose and

85

reached for me. Now I could see its features more clearly. I felt as though I were looking at a photo negative. A walking negative—of a kid about my age.

I could make out a small nose. Glittering eyes. A hot white scar above one brow.

Wait.

I knew this kid!

"Gibson!" I whispered.

"That's right," the thing snarled. "It's me. The real Buddy Gibson. You stole my body from me. And I want it back!"

18

~~~

"This can't be happening!" I moaned.

But it was. The glowing form of Buddy Gibson lurched toward me. I turned to run.

Something tripped me. I fell on my face.

"Give me my body back!" The ghostly voice was stronger than before.

I rolled over onto my back. Buddy Gibson loomed above me. He was easy to recognize now. He looked solid. Terrifyingly real.

He grabbed me by the collar of my pajamas and lifted me off the floor. He was so strong!

"Give it back," he snarled. "Give it back!"

"Please, Buddy. I don't know how this happened!" I tried to explain. "It wasn't me. I didn't do it."

"Liar! You're trying to trick me!" Gibson grinned nastily. "But it won't work."

He held out his hand. He reached toward my chest. Waves of cold flowed over me. He moved his hand closer.

It began to disappear.

It was sinking slowly into my chest!

"What are you doing?" I gasped in horror.

"It's my body!" Gibson cried. "I'm taking it back!"

Panicked, I shoved him with all my might. He must not have been ready for it. He stumbled backward to the floor.

So did I. I scrambled quickly to my feet. Then I got into my karate stance. It was the only thing I could think of.

But Buddy Gibson wasn't getting up. He lay on the floor, thrashing as if he were fighting an invisible enemy. His figure dimmed. Flickered—like a lightbulb that was about to burn out.

Whatever was happening, now was my chance to talk to him. I had to make him understand!

I wiped my face. I was sweating from fear.

"Listen, Gibson," I babbled. "You've got to believe me. I didn't do this on purpose. Someone . . . some*thing* did it to me. I don't know how it happened. I don't want to be here at all. Really!"

Gibson crawled away from me. He raised himself shakily against the wall. He was so dim now that I could barely see him.

"Not strong enough yet," Gibson whispered. "Next time. Next time I'll be stronger. I'll teach you to steal my life from me."

"But—"

Too late. Gibson disappeared.

And I was left standing there in his stupid cowboy pajamas.

I climbed back in bed, pulled the sheet up to my chin, and lay there, shivering. I was wide awake. No way I was going to close my eyes.

I could never stand up to another attack like that. Not if Gibson would be even stronger next time. I *had* to win that game tomorrow.

Before Gibson came back—and finished me off!

19

We boarded the bus the next day for our trip to the big game. The guys were all in high spirits. They clapped each other on the back and said things like "Reety-do!"

Reety-do?

I didn't think I would *ever* get used to this time.

I held my hand up for a high five, but all I got was a blank stare from Johnny Beans.

I took a seat beside Boog. He spent most of the ride bragging about how we were going to clobber the other team.

"We'll murderize them!" he announced. "Right, Buddy?"

"Uh—right," I agreed with a weak grin.

All I could think about was how hard I had to play.

Was it really possible for one guy to make the difference in winning and losing?

What if I couldn't do it?

While the other kids told jokes and laughed, I thought about how this was probably the next to last bus ride for all of us.

It was really depressing.

Finally we arrived. We tumbled off the bus. A big crowd had gathered for the game. The ballpark felt like a county fair. The air was filled with the good smells of hot dogs and hamburgers. Some guy was wandering around selling cotton candy.

We had a little batting practice. Boog slammed one pitch after the other over the fence. He was dead-on! Watching him, I started to feel a little more hopeful. If we all played like him, we might have a chance to turn things around!

I scanned the crowded bleachers. My eye stopped on Ernie, the bus driver. He sat in the top row. A big grin was plastered across his face.

"Be careful what you wish for," I muttered. "You just might get it."

Finally it was time to start. Our two teams lined up on opposite sides of the field while a high school band screeched through what was supposed to be *The Star-Spangled Banner*. The way they played it, it sounded more like a bunch of yowling cats.

After the song, one of the umpires flipped a coin. We won the toss. That meant we were the home team.

And we were up second. The coaches handed in their lineups to the plate umpire and shook hands.

The umpire raised his hand in the air. "Play ball!"

I sucked in a deep breath.

This was it!

By the fifth inning, the score was four to three. We were losing. And I was starting to get really scared.

I kept blowing easy plays. Like when one of the Wildcat batters popped a high one right to me.

"I got it!" I yelled. I danced back and forth as the ball came down. It was an easy out. Until the ball hit the edge of my glove and bounced over the foul line.

My whole team groaned.

"Hold it like a basket, Gibson!" Boog roared at me.

I ran after the ball. My face felt as if it were on fire.

I knew how the game was supposed to end. But I was starting to wonder. What if things didn't go the way they were supposed to? I mean, history was already different—because I wasn't really Buddy Gibson. I was in his body, sure, but how did I know how he would have played the game?

Maybe I had already messed up so badly that there was no way we could win.

Maybe I blew my chance to change history—and get back home.

No! I couldn't think that way!

The Wildcats had a second baseman who was just *amazing* at the plate. He was a skinny, short kid

92

with glasses. But boy, could he swing a bat! No matter what he did, he couldn't help but get a hit.

By the seventh inning, the score was five to three. The Wildcats had two outs and runners on second and third. When the second baseman stepped in the batter's box, I groaned.

I was beginning to seriously hate that kid.

For the next few minutes, Wade, our pitcher, kept hurling strikes right over the inside corner of the plate. But the Wildcat batter kept fouling them off. Wade must have thrown him ten pitches, and the count was still no balls and two strikes.

At last Coach Johnson came trotting out to the mound. We all moved in.

"Walk him," Coach ordered.

"Oh, come on, Coach. I know I can get this guy," Wade protested.

Coach shook his head. "It's not worth it. He's too good. If he gets a hit, it'll be a homer—and then the Wildcats will score three runs. Walk him."

Suddenly I remembered something I'd seen once in a pro game.

"Hey, Coach. I have an idea," I whispered. Quickly I told him my plan.

Coach's eyes flashed. "I like it," he said quietly. He glanced at the catcher, then the pitcher. "Billy? Wade? You're the ones who have to make this work. Do you think you can do it?"

Billy and Wade nodded eagerly.

"Are we going to play ball here?" the umpire yelled.

Coach clapped his hands. "Okay, you heard me," he called loudly. But I saw him wink at Billy and Wade.

I took my base and watched Billy tug his mask back on. He stood behind the plate and held his right hand out wide.

"Are you guys going to chicken out and walk me?" the batter sneered.

"Wait and see," I answered under my breath.

Wade calmly threw the ball way wide of the plate.

"Ball one!" the umpire yelled.

Billy tossed it back.

Calls of "Chicken!" and *"Braawk!"* came from the Wildcats' dugout. Wade ignored them. He threw another way wide and Billy sent it back. Then again. The umpire called ball three.

Now was the time.

"Pay attention, ump," I muttered under my breath.

Billy still held his arm out wide. The batter glanced back at his jeering teammates and laughed. Wade threw again.

But instead of a wide one, he threw a fastball straight down the middle of the plate!

Billy squatted to catch it. The batter never even started his swing. His mouth fell open as the umpire yelled, "Stee-rike three! You're out!"

"Hey, no fair!" the batter yelled. "They can't do that."

Billy tossed the ball to the umpire. "We just did it, Einstein," he retorted. "Side retired."

Whooping with glee, we raced to the dugout. Coach stood grinning. "That was terrific, boys!"

I threw my glove on the bench. I felt much better, even though we were still behind two runs. There was a lot of game left. Plenty of time to make it up.

"Buddy," the coach called. "You're last at bat. Run out to the bus for me, would you? I left a pack of cigarettes on the front seat. Get them for me."

"Sure, Coach," I agreed.

I really should throw them away, I thought. But he would just buy more.

I ran out to the bus quickly. I didn't want to miss the game. As I got there, the doors folded open.

The bus driver must be in there, I thought.

But when I jumped up the steps, I was brought up short by the sight in the driver's seat.

Buddy Gibson!

There he was, right in broad daylight. Waiting for me. He looked strong. Solid. Not like a negative anymore.

"Oh, no!" I gasped.

He grinned.

"Oh, yes," he rasped. "And I'm not going away this time. *You* are!"

20

"**W**ait!" I cried. "You've got to listen to—"

That was all I got out. Then Gibson threw himself at me.

I fell backward. The air whooshed out of my lungs when I hit the ground. Gibson jumped down and sat on my chest. I struggled like crazy, trying to throw him off. But he was too strong.

"I'll teach you, you jerk," he panted. "I'll show you what it's like to be kicked out of your own body!"

He put his hands on my head. I felt the horrible wave of coldness again.

Then his fingers slid into my flesh.

They actually dipped into my skull!

"Noooo!" I yelled.

Icy fingers probed at my brain. Numbness stole over me. The world started to go dark.

This is it! I thought. I've had it!

Then I guess Buddy Gibson and I . . . merged.

It was the weirdest thing I ever experienced. All at once, I felt—bigger. Stronger. Faster.

I flexed my fingers. My hands felt as if I'd just taken off a pair of thick gloves.

For the first time, I really fit into Gibson's body.

I lay there on my back, breathing deeply. Energy pulsed through me.

Suddenly I felt a jolt of panic. Somehow I knew it wasn't coming from me.

"You're really from the future?" Gibson's voice gasped. *"And we're really going to be in a bus crash this afternoon?"*

His voice echoed off the inside of my skull. It wasn't a very comfortable feeling.

But at least I finally got someone to believe me!

"That's right. We all die—unless we win this game," I told him. I spoke out loud. It just seemed like the thing to do.

He didn't say anything. I couldn't tell whether he was even still in there.

"Gibson? Are you still there?" I asked.

There was no answer.

I climbed cautiously to my feet and brushed myself off.

From the distance I heard Boog shout, "Get a move on, Buddy!"

The game! I grabbed the coach's cigarettes and ran.

Maybe Gibson believed me. Maybe he didn't—and he was going to try to get me again.

But I couldn't worry about him now.

I still had a game to win!

21

~

I raced back to the ball field. "What's up?" I asked Johnny Beans.

"We got our third out already," he told me, shaking his head. "This game isn't going so well."

I grabbed my glove and hustled out to third base. I felt nervous. Antsy. I stalked around my base. "Come on, hit it my way," I muttered.

What was going on? I didn't usually feel like this.

"Wake up, man!" a voice snapped in my head. *"We've got to win this game!"*

"Gibson!" I exclaimed.

"No, it's the tooth fairy. Of course it's me! What, did you think I was going to skip the big game?"

He was still with me! Right there in my head!

At least he wasn't attacking me.

Not yet anyway.

"Heads up!" Gibson yelled. I jumped and glanced around wildly.

The ball whizzed past, near second base. A line drive. Straight to the hole in our outfield. This was bad. The Wildcats could get a triple.

Then I saw Boog. He raced across the field as if his shoes were on fire. He dove—and scooped the ball with his glove just before it hit the ground.

"Do it, Boog!" I yelled. What a play!

For the rest of the inning, Gibson kept quiet. I didn't know whether he was there inside me or not. But I didn't have much time to worry about it. I had to concentrate on the game!

At the top of the ninth, the score was five to three. We had two outs, and runners on first and second. I was on deck.

Then Billy Fein singled. Bases were loaded, and I was up.

As I stepped to home plate, I felt a surge of determination. I swung the bat and stared out at the pitcher.

I knew, I *knew* I was going to nail it.

That was Gibson inside me, I realized suddenly. He had a kind of confidence I'd never felt before. But I could feel it now.

He was working with me! Helping me!

The pitcher came at me with a hanging curveball. I grinned and clobbered that sucker.

I didn't even bother to watch it. I just tossed the bat aside and trotted the bases.

"Grand slam homer!" Boog roared from the dugout. "Gib-son! Gib-son!"

The batter after me struck out. Our side was retired. "So what?" Boog remarked as we trotted out to the field. "We're two runs up. The trophy is ours!"

But I knew differently. I remembered Ernie telling me how Shadyside led by two in the bottom of the ninth.

Just the way it was now.

History was repeating itself!

"Don't start celebrating yet," I cautioned.

"Win. We have to win!" said the voice in my head.

Gibson was so determined. It was like a fire inside me. I felt powerful. Alive.

But would it be enough? Would it change history?

And would that save the team and get me home?

22

The bottom of the ninth didn't start out well. Wade was tired, I guess. Anyway, the first Wildcat batter—that skinny second baseman with the glasses—hit a triple on the first pitch.

I winced. Not good. Definitely not good.

The next batter singled. So did the one after that. But at least I was able to keep the runner at third from going home.

The bases were loaded. Just the way Ernie described it.

The next batter stepped up. He hefted the bat with his left hand.

My stomach did a flip. "This is it," I said. "This is where it all happens!"

"Shut up and look sharp," Gibson warned in my head.

I was too scared to get annoyed.

I hugged the third baseline, but the rest of the team shifted over toward right field. "Move it, Buddy!" Coach Johnson yelled.

I ignored him.

"Buddy!" he yelled again.

I waved at him, but I didn't budge.

Coach called time and ran over to me.

"What do you think you're doing?" he demanded.

Oh, boy.

"I'm playing third," I replied, trying to sound innocent.

"I see. Are you playing third on my team?"

I gulped. "Uh—yes, sir."

"So why don't you move where I tell you to move?" he barked.

"He's going to push the ball to the left, Coach. I just know it," I argued.

"Oh, you know it, do you?" Coach snapped. "How do you know? Do you have a crystal ball or something?"

"Kind of," I mumbled.

"Oh, for Pete's sake." Coach sounded disgusted. "If you're not moving toward right in three seconds, I'll take you out of the game!"

I groaned, but I moved. What else could I do? I

stood there halfway to second, gazing tensely at that third base line.

The runners took their leads. The guy on second took such a big jump, he ended up only a few feet away from me.

The second the pitcher threw, I sprinted to the right.

WHAP! The batter cracked a line drive straight down the baseline.

"Go!" Gibson yelled in my head.

The ball screamed through the air. I'd never reach it! I'd never make it.

But then something swelled inside me. It couldn't get by. It *wouldn't* get by!

I leapt through the air. My arm stretched out so far, I thought my shoulder was going to pop.

"I got it!" I screamed.

The ball hit the tip of my glove.

And stuck. I squeezed my fingers around it.

One out!

It had seemed such a sure base hit, the runner was already halfway home. He turned and tore back toward third. From the ground, I reached out and slapped the base with my glove.

Double play. Two out!

Feet skidded behind me. Still flat on the ground, I rolled back toward second. The runner from second spun to go back. I rolled twice in the dirt and tagged the heel of his shoe.

Three out!

A triple play!

The game was over. And we won!

The crowd in the bleachers erupted in a huge roar. I lay there, staring up at the sky.

"Yes!" I screamed. "Yes!"

My teammates raced to me from all directions. They pulled me to my feet and then hoisted me onto their shoulders. We paraded around the field as the crowd cheered.

Boog was jumping up and down like an idiot. "An unassisted triple play! Did you see that?" he yelled to the whole world.

I was still dazed from what I did. What *we* did. Buddy Gibson and I. An unassisted triple play!

I went through the trophy ceremony in a daze of happiness and relief. In fact, it wasn't until I was on my second burger at the barbecue that it hit me.

Hold on a second!

"What am I still doing here?" I gasped.

"What's wrong?" Gibson asked inside my head.

"I'm still here," I muttered. "That's what's wrong! On TV the time traveler gets to leave after he does what he's supposed to do. What's the deal?"

Boog, who was standing nearby, turned and stared at me.

"Are you talking to me?" he asked.

"Uh—no," I said quickly. "I just said, 'What a meal!' There's so much to eat!"

"Yeah. Isn't it great?" Boog laughed and stuffed half a hot dog into his mouth.

"Maybe this doesn't work like TB," Gibson suggested.

"TV," I said under my breath.

"Whatever. What I'm saying is, maybe you can't go home." Gibson's voice was unusually quiet, for him. *"Maybe you're stuck here. With me."*

"You think?" My heart sank. "No. It can't be. There must be some delay or something. That's all."

"I hope so," he said. *"But just in case—are you any good at schoolwork?"*

I had to laugh.

Boog gave me a strange look. "What's so funny?" he asked.

"Oh, nothing," I answered.

"Come on, boys. Loading up," Coach Johnson called.

We all climbed on the bus. Soon it was whizzing down the road and we were on our way home. Everybody but me.

I closed my eyes. Maybe I even drifted off. Because I don't remember how long we'd been on the bus when it stalled.

Hrrrn, hrrnn, hrrrrrnnn, the starter moaned.

I sat up, bleary-eyed. "What is it?" I asked Boog.

"The bus is stalled," he answered.

The noise of the starter continued. "Don't flood it," Coach Johnson advised.

I peered sleepily out the window. Then I stared in horror.

A double thread of track ran below the bus and curved sharply to the right.

We were stalled on the railroad tracks!

My plan—it didn't work! We were all going to die anyway!

"We have to get out!" I yelled. *"Now!"*

"Simmer down, son," Ernie called. "It'll start in a minute."

"No. The train. The train!" I wailed. "It's going to hit us. Why won't you—" I broke off. Listening.

Oh, no. *No!*

The train's rumble came right through the floor of the bus.

"The train! It's coming!" Johnny Beans screeched.

"Oh, no!" Coach shouted. "Ernie, get us out of here!"

The starter whined. I could see the light from the train now.

"Let us out!" someone screamed.

But there was no time. The train barreled around the curve. Its light blared in my face.

We were done for!

23

"No!" I yelled.

It couldn't be! Not after I'd been through so much!

HRRRN! HRRRRN! The engine whined. The train roared closer. Its whistle shrieked.

Then the engine caught. The bus lurched and surged forward.

WHAM! Metal crunched as the train clipped the rear corner of the bus. We shot forward as if the bus were a rocket.

Ernie struggled with the wheel. The bus careened crazily back and forth across the road.

"Hold on, everybody!" he bellowed.

We were all yelling and screaming now. The smell of burning rubber filled my nose. I clutched the metal bar across the top of the seat desperately.

Then the bus ran off the road. I lost my grip and went flying. My head crashed against the window.

And that's the last thing I remember.

"Buddy? Buddy? Are you okay?"

I opened my eyes and saw the coach—*my* coach, Mr. Burress—looking down at me. I glimpsed Eve's face over his shoulder. Her mouth hung open so wide, you could have fit a baseball in there.

"All right!" I whispered.

I was back!

Coach Burress helped me to my feet.

"Send in Charlotte to pinch-run," he called over his shoulder.

"I'm okay. I'll shake it off," I protested.

"Shake it off? You just got clobbered in the head with a fastball. You're out of this game," Coach declared firmly.

Coach and Eve led me to the dugout. On the way, I gazed around, drinking in the sights. Red and blue uniforms that didn't look like sacks. Women in jeans instead of dresses. Normal cars.

I was really back!

"So—what did I miss?" I asked Eve, trying to sound casual.

"Miss?" Eve frowned. "You were knocked out for only about fifteen seconds. You didn't miss anything."

We reached the dugout. Both my mom and dad were there already, hovering. Mom dipped a cloth in the ice chest and held it to the place where the ball had got me.

"Mom, I'm all right, really," I told her.

She smoothed my hair back and gave me a worried look. "Are you sure, Buddy?"

"Yeah." I grinned. "I have a hard head."

Then I did something really embarrassing. I threw my arms around my mom and dad and hugged them both. Hard.

"My goodness!" Mom sounded surprised. "Thank you, sweetie! What brought that on?"

I flushed. "I don't know," I mumbled. "I just felt like it."

Mom glanced at Dad and raised her eyebrows. "Maybe we'd better take him to the doctor after all."

After I talked them out of that, I sat on the bench and watched Oneiga clobber us. Same old lousy Shadyside team.

Boy, was I glad to see them!

By the time we left the ball field though, I was starting to wonder. Everything here was so real. So normal. And even though I spent three days in 1948, it seemed that no time passed at all in the present.

Did I really travel in time?

Or did I just imagine it all?

Maybe the whole adventure happened in my mind!

I puzzled over it as Dad drove us toward Shadyside.

110

Eve was riding with us—her parents couldn't make it to the game.

We stopped off at the 7-Eleven on Village Road. Dad ran in for sodas. When he came back to the car, he tossed a couple of packs of baseball cards onto the backseat.

"Maybe that'll help make up for losing the game," he said.

I smiled. "Thanks, Dad."

"Yeah, thanks, Mr. Sanders," Eve echoed.

I picked up one of the packets and tore off the plastic wrapper. Eve leaned over to watch. "Get anything good?"

My mouth dropped in shock as I spotted the top card. It was a special issue on shiny, stiff paper with a gold border. A special Hall of Famer card.

Staring out at me was Buddy Gibson!

He looked older, of course. But it was definitely him. No way could I make a mistake about that. The caption said he played third base for the Yankees in the sixties.

"Oh, man!" Eve exclaimed. "A Buddy Gibson! You're so lucky. Those things are pretty rare."

I studied the card with a pounding heart.

So it wasn't a dream at all!

I *did* go back in time. I *did* change the past. No one died in that bus crash. And Buddy Gibson went on to the major leagues. To the Hall of Fame!

"Buddy Gibson." Eve sighed. "The most famous person who ever came from Shadyside. I sure would like to meet him. But he probably wouldn't have any time for a couple of kids."

I grinned. "I have a feeling he'd find time for us."

Because, thanks to me, Buddy Gibson had all the time in the world!

Are you ready for another walk
down Fear Street?
Turn the page for a terrifying
sneak preview.

R·L·STINE'S

GHOSTS OF FEAR STREET ® #23

WHY I'M NOT AFRAID
OF GHOSTS

Coming mid-July 1997

Robbie felt exhausted as he climbed the attic stairs. He was so tired he couldn't even float up.

He couldn't remember feeling this tired before.

He began the night with so much energy. Now he had almost zero. He didn't have enough energy to be bothered when his sister danced around the attic taunting him.

He was too tired to care!

"Mr. High and Frighty," Dora teased. "What a terrible ghost you are!"

"Cut it out," Robbie moaned. "Just shut up." He slumped in the armchair, so weak he couldn't even raise dust.

Dora did a little tapdance. "Don't you worry, Mr. Useless Excuse for a Nightmare!"

"Don't worry? Even *you* can't scare Oliver Bowen. Nothing works," Robbie mumbled. "We've tried everything we usually do."

Dora grinned. "Right. So it's time for something completely different. Let's follow Oliver to school—and haunt him out in the open, in front of other kids!"

What a mean plan!

Robbie felt so encouraged and happy, he even managed to smile.

Both ghosts clung to Oliver's shadow as he went inside the big redbrick school next morning. There were so many students in the halls that Robbie was confused. He hadn't seen this many people in one place in a long time! If ever—outside of TV.

Oliver's first class was English. Robbie was relieved to get to a room where they could stay still for a while. It was hard following Oliver when he dodged between people. This school was huge and noisy!

Dora didn't start anything yet. Robbie wondered if something was the matter with her.

Maybe she was just trying to get used to being in this big building! It felt strange to be outside the house.

By the end of Oliver's class, Robbie began feeling better. More himself. Dora seemed to perk up too.

Oliver's second class was math. Robbie found it

easier navigating the halls this time. Dora winked at him. She must be ready for the big scare, Robbie thought.

The teacher, Mr. Gerard, handed out a math test. "Now that we've gotten the introductory material out of the way, I want to see where you all are in math. We have some new faces in Shadyside this year." He smiled at Oliver.

Oliver smiled, looking embarrassed. He peeked at the kids near him. Robbie checked them out too. They were studying Oliver. He was the new kid, after all.

"Oh, yeah," Dora murmured. "This will be good. Now everybody's looking at him."

Dora clasped her hands above her head and shook them like a champion. Robbie rolled his eyes.

"Here's an extra sheet of paper," Mr. Gerard continued, passing out blank paper to all the kids. "Remember, show your calculations, everyone!"

Some kids groaned and mumbled that it was too hard, but Robbie noticed Oliver went right at it. Oliver must be good at math.

Oliver was breezing through the third problem when Dora sprang into action. She grabbed the pencil out of his hand. She zoomed up and drilled the pencil point-first into the ceiling.

Oliver blinked, stared at his paper and his hand.

He peered down at the floor.

No pencil.

But also, no reaction. Oliver didn't seem to think anything was wrong.

Robbie knew what Dora's mistake was. She performed the pencil trick so fast Oliver didn't even know what had happened!

Oliver yawned into the back of his hand, dragged out his backpack, and pulled out his three-ring binder.

He flipped it open and took another pencil out of the pocket in front. Then he went back to work.

"Do it slower," Robbie suggested. "He has to be able to see where it goes."

"Shut up!" Dora snapped.

But Robbie noticed that she did what he said. For once.

She grabbed Oliver's pencil slowly this time. She waved it around in front of his eyes to make sure he was watching what she was doing, then zapped it up into the ceiling. It hung quivering next to the other pencil.

Oliver stared at the two pencils for a second.

Then he got out another one and went back to work.

Dora's mouth dropped open. So did Robbie's.

"How can he ignore those pencils? Doesn't he even think it's weird?" Dora demanded. Robbie shrugged.

Dora tried again. But this time, Oliver clutched his pencil so tight Dora couldn't snatch it away!

"Let go!" she screeched in frustration. Since she couldn't get the pencil away, she jiggled it so Oliver scribbled on his math paper.

He frowned and erased the squiggles.

And went back to work!

By this time, Robbie noticed, other kids were peeking at Oliver. The girl at the desk to Oliver's right sat staring at the pencils in the ceiling, her mouth open. The boy to Oliver's left narrowed his eyes, glancing from the pencils to Oliver and back.

Robbie tried to send a mental message to Oliver. *Just act scared,* Robbie ordered him. *Act scared and we'll leave you alone!*

Oliver ignored the ceiling pencils, the other kids, and Robbie's thoughts, and went on working.

Robbie could tell Dora was really steamed now! She snatched Oliver's notebook off his desk and slammed it onto the floor!

Mr. Gerard looked up. Several heads whipped around.

"Uh," Oliver mumbled. "Sorry."

He leaned over to pick up his notebook. Dora grabbed his third pencil and shot it into the ceiling!

Oliver just got out another one.

Robbie shook his head. How can Oliver stay so calm? he wondered.

The girl next to Oliver gasped. "But—but—" she stammered, pointing at the ceiling.

"What?" Oliver asked. He glanced up. "Oh." He

shrugged and gazed back down at his test. He studied the next problem on his paper, chewing on his pencil.

All the kids in the class stared at him. One or two giggled.

The boy to Oliver's left leaned over. "How did you *do* that?" the boy whispered.

Yeah, Oliver, Robbie thought, explain that one.

Oliver just smiled mysteriously and went back to work.

The room buzzed as the class muttered and murmured. Some kids pointed at the pencils in the ceiling.

"Class!" Mr. Gerard exclaimed. "What's all this noise? Get back to work!"

The kids stopped whispering. They bent over their math tests. They picked up their pencils and went back to work.

But everyone kept sneaking looks at Oliver.

No one could concentrate!

Dora swooped at Oliver's desk. She grabbed his math test and tugged it.

Oliver dropped his pencil on the desk and grabbed his test. Dora snatched his fourth pencil and jammed it into the ceiling!

Oliver sighed.

"Coo-uhl!" the boy on Oliver's left exclaimed.

Robbie couldn't believe it. All Oliver did was

open his notebook and reach into his Ziploc pencil keeper. He wasn't scared at all!

But this time Oliver's pencil keeper was empty.

He glanced at the girl next to him. She shook her head no.

He peeked at the boy to his left. Another head shake.

Oliver sighed again and stood up. He gazed at the pencils in the ceiling. He climbed onto his desk chair and reached for them.

"Oliver Bowen, exactly *what* do you think you're doing?" Mr. Gerard demanded.

That was when Dora did her worst. Or best, depending on how you looked at it, Robbie thought.

She grabbed Oliver and spun him around on the chair!

Robbie clutched his stomach. Oliver twirled so fast! If *he* was spun like that, he knew he would throw up.

Robbie flew up to the ceiling as the class went wild. Kids jumped to their feet. The whole room buzzed with their exclamations: "Wow!" "No way!" "How does he do that?" "Oh, man!" "Teach me to do that!"

Mr. Gerard tried to restore order. "Oliver Bowen!" he shouted. "Stop that! Oliver Bowen! Do I have to send you to the principal's office? Class! Settle down!" He hit his desk with a steel ruler.

Still the kids pointed, talked, and stared.

Dora spun Oliver six times. Then she let go of him.

Robbie gazed at his sister. She was fading. Her outline was beginning to blur. She used up a lot of energy moving something as big as a boy! She looked a little green.

But what about Oliver? Did Dora's haunting work? Was he afraid? Robbie turned to face him.

Oliver swayed on his chair, trying to steady himself.

He opened his eyes really wide.

And his mouth!

His face twisted.

Dora had done it, Robbie realized.

Oliver was going to scream!

About R.L. Stine

R.L. Stine, the creator of *Ghosts of Fear Street,* has written almost 100 scary novels for kids. The *Ghosts of Fear Street* series, like the *Fear Street* series, takes place in Shadyside and centers on the scary events that happen to people on Fear Street.

When he isn't writing, R.L. Stine likes to play pinball on his very own pinball machine, and explore New York City with his wife, Jane, his teenage son, Matt, and his dog, Nadine.

WIN A TRIP TO MEET

R.L. STINE

...IF YOU DARE!

You could win an exciting weekend in New York City and have lunch with R.L. Stine

---

1 GRAND PRIZE: A WEEKEND (3 DAY/2 NIGHT) TRIP TO NEW YORK CITY TO MEET R.L. STINE

10 First Prizes: Walkman and an autographed "Ghosts of Fear Street" Audiobook

20 Second Prizes: Autographed "Ghosts of Fear Street" T-Shirt

30 Third Prizes: Autographed "Ghosts of Fear Street" Audiobook

50 Fourth Prizes: Autographed "Ghosts of Fear Street" Book

100 Fifth Prizes: "Ghosts of Fear Street" Sticker

Complete the official entry form and send to:
Pocket Books, GOFS Sweepstakes
1230 Avenue of the Americas, New York, NY 10020

Name_____(Child)

Birthdate_____/_____/_____

Name_____(Parent)

Address _____

City_____State_____Zip_____

Phone (_____)_____

See back for official rules

1302 (1 of 2)

POCKET BOOKS/"GOFS AUDIO" SWEEPSTAKES
Sweepstakes Official Rules:

1. No Purchase Necessary. Enter by mailing the completed Official Entry Form (no copies allowed) or by mailing a 3" x 5" card with your name and address to the Pocket Books/GOFS Sweepstakes, 13th Floor, 1230 Avenue of the Americas, NY, NY 10020. Entries must be received by 6/30/97. Not responsible for lost, late, stolen, illegible, mutilated, incomplete, postage due or misdirected entries or mail or for typographical errors in the entry form or rules. Enter as often as you wish, but one entry per envelope. Winners will be selected at random from all eligible entries received in a drawing to be held on or about 7/1/97.

2. Prizes: One Grand Prize: A weekend (three day/two night) trip for up to four persons (the winning minor, one parent or legal guardian and two guests) including round-trip coach airfare from the major U.S. airport nearest the winner's residence to New York City, ground transportation or car rental in New York City, meals, two nights in a hotel (one room, occupancy for four) and lunch with R.L. Stine (approx. retail value $3500.000, trip must be taken on the date specified by Simon & Schuster, Inc.), Ten First Prizes: Walkman and Autographed "Ghosts of Fear Street" Audiobook (approx. retail value $40.00) Twenty Second Prizes: Autographed "Ghosts of Fear Street" T-shirt (approx. retail value $20.00 each), Thirty Third Prizes: Autographed "Ghosts of Fear Street" Audiobook (approx. retail value $7.95 each), Fifty Fourth Prizes: Autographed "Ghosts of Fear Street" Book (approx. retail value: $3.99) One Hundred Fifth Prizes: "Ghosts of Fear Street" Sticker (approx. retail value: $1.00)

3. The sweepstakes is open to residents of the U.S. and Canada, excluding Quebec, not older than fourteen as of 6/30/97. Proof of age required to claim prize. Prizes will be awarded to the winner's parent or legal guardian. Void in Puerto Rico and wherever prohibited or restricted by law. Simon & Schuster, Inc., Parachute Press, Inc., their respecitve officers, directors, shareholders, employees, suppliers, parents, subsidiaries, affiliates, agencies, sponsors, participating retailers, and persons connected with the use, marketing or conduct of this sweepstakes and their families living in the same household, are not eligible.

4. One prize per person or household. Prizes are not transferable and may not be substituted except by sponsor, in event of unavailability, in which case a prize of equal or greater value will be awarded. All prizes will be awarded. The odds of winning a prize depend upon the number of eligible entries received.

5. If a winner is a Canadian resident, then he/she must correctly answer a skill-based question administered by mail.

6. All expenses on receipt and use of prize including Federal, state and local taxes are the sole responsibility of the winners. Winners will be notified by mail. Winners may be required to execute and return an Affidavit of Eligibility and Release and all other legal documents which the sweepstakes sponsor may require (including a W-9 tax form) within 15 days of receipt of notification or an alternate winner will be selected.

7. Winners irrevocably grant Pocket Books, Parachute Press, Inc. and Simon & Schuster Audio the worldwide right, for no additional consideration, to use their names, photographs, likenesses, and entries for any advertising, promotion, marketing and publicity purposes relating to this promotional contest or otherwise without further compensation to or permission from the entrants, except where prohibited by law.

8. Winners agree that Simon & Schuster Inc., Parachute Press, Inc., their respective officers, directors, shareholders, employees, suppliers, parents, subsidiaries, affiliates, agencies, sponsors, participating retailers, and persons connected with the use, marketing or conduct of this sweepstakes, shall have no liability in connection with the collection, acceptance or use of the prizes awarded herein.

9. By participating in this sweepstakes, entrants agree to be bound by these rules and the decisions of the judges and sweepstakes sponsors, which are final in all matters relating to the sweepstakes.

10. For a list of major prize winners, (available after 7/11/97) send a stamped, self-addressed envelope to Prize Winners, Pocket Books/GOFS Sweepstakes, 13th Floor, 1230 Avenue of the Americas, NY, NY 10020.